Dedication

For my dearest Rose, Tom and Joe
and my six fabulous grandchildren.

And for our dearly missed Bunty,
who is in heaven chasing rabbits.

Deb Mawson

Ogo Pogo Saves The Day

Written and illustrated by
Deb Mawson

First published 2020

ISBN 978-1-9161978-8-6

Print production by
Gipping Press Ltd: Unit 2, Lion Barn Estate,
Needham Market, Suffolk, IP6 8NZ
Tel: 01449 721599
www.gippingpress.co.uk

Acknowledgements

In deep gratitude to Marie for my beautiful winters in that old Portugese house on the cliff top, where I discover that less is more.

Thanks again to the fabulous Gipping Press and to Catherine aka 'Pernickety Kate' - my editor.

To Framlingham
Kettleburgh
Parham
Thorpeness
Snape
Little Japan
Aldeburgh
Blaxhall
Iken
Slaughden
Aldeburgh yacht club
Martello Tower
The Woods
Butley
Butley Mills
R Alde
Orford
Orford Lighthouse
Orford Ness
Orford Beach
To Nacton
R ORE
W
N
E
Shingle Street

Chapter 1

Midsummer can be one of the most positive and inspiring times of the year. Between the 20th and 22nd of June, in our country, the longest day and the shortest night arrive. Long hours of beautiful daylight made more lovely by the fullness of nature – birds, flowers and sunshine. These days are known as the turning of the year. However, we never feel we have reached anywhere like the middle of the summer – or had enough of it. When this day dawned, Saturday June 20th, 2020 (all the twos), that date in itself made it special.

This very early morning in Kettleburgh, Suffolk, as the sun crept up over the horizon, the two cousins, Bella and Ellie, stirred in their sleep in their bunk beds. Both of these cousins have their birthdays at midsummer. Ellie has hers one day before Bella's.

The clock light went on at exactly 7.00 a.m. Bella and Ellie both woke up at almost the same moment with an immediate sense of excitement and anticipation, knowing it was to be their special day.

Bella hung over the top bunk to see if Ellie was awake in the bunk below. Ellie was yawning and stretching.

Bella slipped out of her bunk down the ladder and signalled to Ellie. 'Shh, come on!' she whispered.

Each one stripped off their pyjamas and pulled on a pair of leggings, T-shirt and a hoody top, then they crept out into the passage. There was a streaky golden, amber and turquoise dawning light coming through the landing window from outside. The two cousins tiptoed down the stairs. They didn't want to wake Bella's parents, Tom and Dee Dee. Seeing the breakfast things laid out on the table, Bella shook out a handful of raisins, and chewing a couple, put the rest into her hoody pocket. For good measure, she opened the jar of dried apricots and pulling out several, handed them to Ellie, who popped one in her mouth and the rest in her pocket. Slipping on their trainers at the back door, Bella then opened the door, beckoning Ellie to follow.

As they stepped outside, they caught their breaths. A low mist lay over the grass all around them, the golden sun filtering down in slanting rays, sparkling onto the dewy grass. The birds were chattering and chirruping, twittering and calling, from branches of the trees around them. The whole garden was ringing with bird music. There was a fragrance of flowers and grass as the sun gradually warmed the earth.

'Wow!' whispered Bella, 'it's our birthday celebrations today – you're 5 and I'm 6! And I'm SO excited already!'

Ellie drew in a breath as she looked around her, and gave a huge grin. Steady, bright, good natured and happy, she felt enormously pleased to have reached the age of 5. She was the youngest of all six cousins and was at last beginning to feel like she was really getting somewhere – catching

3

them up! Bella, turning 6, was strong, fearless, determined and happy to speak her mind!

The two cousins sprinted across the grass and clambered over the wooden gate into the field beyond. To the left of the gate, near the ditch, stood the beautiful old oak tree; Bella's favourite tree in her whole garden. An ancient tree, standing large and proud. Growing there for several hundreds of years, it was the tree where, around the base, the first snowdrops appeared in January. In late Autumn, the crisp golden oak leaves were the last to drift, and the little acorns in their cups fell into the field.

That oak tree was where all of the six cousins, with Magic Joe, had landed to hide in the garden in part of their adventure exactly a year ago. Bella and Ellie had such strong memories of riding on the backs of those two beautiful geese, Alberta and Nova, and landing next to the tree. The rescuing of their dear Ogo Pogo in the magic box; that was something they would never forget.

They circuited round to the back of the trunk, and peered down the rabbit hole hidden in the roots. This was the place Bella came to every morning to feed the wild rabbits. The ones her parents were so keen to keep out of the garden and off their flower and vegetable patches!

'Come on, bunnies,' Bella called quietly. 'It's breakfast time!'

'Yes, come on out, bunnies!' whispered Ellie. 'We've got you some apricots and raisins!'

Taking the raisins out of her pocket, Bella

sprinkled a few around the hole at the roots of the tree. Ellie pulled out two apricots, and hesitating, put one near the raisins, and popped the other in her mouth. Bella starting giggling. They sat back on their knees and waited.

An ancient tree standing large and proud

The two children's eyes were glued to the hole. Waiting and watching. But as they did so, a strange thing happened. The rabbit hole seemed to start growing. Bella and Ellie looked at it, their eyes widening in disbelief.

'Wow! What's going on?' whispered Ellie. 'That hole's getting bigger... look, it's growing!'

Then all at once, there began a small feeling of a tugging at the children's arms. The pulling sensation seemed to be coming from the rabbit hole in the base of the tree. It felt really weird, as if something was trying to suck them down the hole. The feeling grew and spread until the whole of their upper bodies felt as if they were being tugged. It was so strong and there was no way of stopping it. Ellie, who was a little nearer to the entrance to the hole, began to disappear arms and head first into it. The hole was now looking like a small circular window – but still growing.

'Ooh, stoppit! Bella, help me, make it stop!' Ellie cried, her voice becoming indistinct and muffled as her head and shoulders disappeared into the dark hole.

'What's going on!?' cried Bella. 'Come back Ellie!' But before she knew it, Ellie's legs were disappearing from view in front of her and Bella was also being pulled and tugged into the hole head first. *'Ew, this feels horrible,'* thought Bella. *'I feel a bit like I'm being sucked up by an invisible, giant, silent hoover. Any minute now we're going to see a white rabbit in a waistcoat, and my name will be Alice!'*

As her head shoulders, arms and legs were pulled down the hole, the space was too low to stand up in, so she had absolutely no choice but to start crawling on her hands and knees into the warm darkening tunnel.

8

Chapter 2

Ellie was trying hard not to cry, not to scream. She didn't like the sucking sensation one bit. 'Help! Help! Bella are you there?'

It reassured her, but only a little, when she heard Bella calling to her from somewhere back in the tunnel, 'I'm coming Ellie, I'm right behind you!'

'Can you make it stop, Bella?' cried Ellie.

'No! I'm being sucked along too,' shouted a breathless Bella from behind.

The two girls were being pulled along, the sucking sensation making them crawl on all fours along the tunnel full of twists and turns. It was nearly completely dark now. The floor of the tunnel was made of warm dry earthy sawdust and old leaf. It didn't hurt them at all. But they couldn't stand up. It was quiet as they shuffled along. There was a musky, warm smell which was not unpleasant, but still not a bit as nice as being outside in the fresh air. The pulling, the crawling seemed to go on for ages.

'Ellie! Are you OK? Are you there? Keep calling back to me so I know you're there!' shouted Bella.

'I'm here, Bella!' called Ellie, 'but I can't stop – it's like something's pulling me!'

'Me too!' replied Bella. And then a few moments later: 'Are you still OK Ellie?'

'Er yes… Are you?'

And so it went on, the little cousins calling

to one another, being pulled along by this invisible suction.

Ellie was just wondering how long she would have to keep crawling like this when she began to see a slight lightening of the tunnel ahead of her. The tunnel turned a corner, still sucking her along, and then began to open up slightly, becoming wider and larger, until she felt just about able to stand. She got up. Just ahead of her in the dim light, she could make out a small door. As her eyes adjusted, she could see that the light was coming from around the door through the cracks, throwing little beams into the tunnel they were in.

As suddenly as the sucking sensation had begun, it stopped. All at once, the girls felt a lightness as the feeling ceased.

'Phew!' called Bella. 'It's stopped!'

Ellie looked around and there was Bella scrabbling to stand right behind her.

'Look!' said Ellie. 'We've reached a door! What shall we do Bella?'

It was a heavy old wooden door with a small circular ringed handle made of rusty iron. It looked ancient and thick, but small - about the size of the chicken house door in Ellie's garden back at home.

They glanced into the dark tunnel behind them and shuddered at the thought of trying to go back that way.

Cautiously Bella leaned forward next to Ellie and twisted the handle, which turned rather creakily. Bella gave the door a shove. It pushed open heavily, and as it did so, both of the children gave a gasp at the sight in front of them.

Chapter 3

There was a circular room, full of a golden light. It was like a small cave but entirely made from a hole in the tree roots. Warm sunshine spread from the other side of the room which was open to the air. The girls stepped inside to have a better look, and shut the door behind them.

To the right side of the room, near the cave opening, was a small fireplace, with a little blackened old kettle and a small saucepan in the hearth. The fireplace was made from a dip in the earth floor. . Some dry kindling - twigs and small pieces of bark lay ready to light in the little fire pit. A wooden bench with mossy cushions was placed nearby it.

In the centre of the room there was a table made of a large circular flat tree stump, and four small tree stump stools around it. On the table were some cups and saucers of walnut shells and pieces of bark. A tiny wooden bowl was on the table with some hazel nuts in it. A few raspberries were in another bowl. A wooden jug with some rosebay willow herb flowers sat on the table.

On the other side of the room, along the left-hand wall, was a little truckle bed covered in a blanket made of woven grasses and moss. There were shelves above, with interesting-looking natural objects stacked along them - pine cones, beautiful feathers, shells, unusual coloured pebbles, crystals, and small dishes made of bark or wood. which was just like a delightful play room - so tidy, comfortable and warm!

But the thing which drew the children's attention most was the golden space beyond.

Bella and Ellie walked past the table to the sunny opening and looked out of the mouth of the tree cave.

'Oh WOW!' they both exclaimed.

They felt a surge of excitement and joy as they looked. There in front of them was… azure blue water!

The side of the room opened out onto a golden sandy beach – a tiny cove. Fine yellow sand, with a covering of various tiny jewel-like shells, greeted them. The beach was still and bright, with blue water lapping in the morning early sunshine. Protected on two sides by sandy cliffs and a steep grassy hill behind, it was completely private and hidden. Nothing could be heard but the songs of the early morning calling birds and a couple of crying seagulls overhead.

'Is that the sea?' asked Ellie in a hushed voice.

'Well, I'm not sure,' replied Bella. 'It could be a river, it could be sea, or could it be a lake?'

Now, these cousins were both used to swimming. They swam every week with their parents in nearby swimming pools, without armbands now, and in the summer time they swam in the mornings when they stayed with their granny Gar Gar by the sea. They were great dippers! To them, it would be just the most natural thing in the world to jump in the water.

'Let's go for a swim!' giggled Ellie. 'Come on Bella, it's our birthdays!'

Before they knew it, they had stripped off, dumped their clothes and shoes on the beach, had run into the rippling waves and were splashing about in the delicious clear water. Laughing and giggling, they played around in the early sunshine. Little rainbow fishes swam by them in shoals and they saw a couple of star fishes lazily sunning themselves on some rocks to the side of the cove. In the rock pools, too, glistened pretty pink anemones, green mossy seaweed, sea urchins and wonderful pearly sea snails. It was just the best birthday swim ever.

'Let's go for a swim!' Giggled Ellie.

After a while, they waded out, and drying themselves off with their hoodies, put their leggings and T shirts back on. Placing their hoodies on a rock to dry in the sunshine, and their trainers nearby, they padded barefoot back into the sunny root-cave and looked around.

'Now what shall we do?'

Chapter 4

Bella was just thinking about eating some of the raspberries that were on the table when there was a WHOOSH and flashing wings appeared from the sky! A large white seagull landed on the small deck behind them. And there, sitting on the top of the bird, like a little jockey, was a small, cheerful-looking pixie boy. He had a mass of sticky out black hair, brown sparkling eyes, funny pointy ears and a dirty face! Wearing a pair of rather tatty trousers made of laurel leaves and a jacket of woven grass, he carried a shoulder bag, also made from two leaves stitched together. He had turned-up little shoes. The pixie boy was about 20 centimetres tall. With a big smile and a cheeky expression, he looked very pleased to see the children. He clapped his hands merrily.

'Hallooo there, you two!' shouted the little fellow.

'Oooh, Magic Joe! It's you! Hurray!' cried Ellie, delighted. 'And look Bella, it's Ray the seagull! Hello Ray!'

And sure enough, there they were, Magic Joe and Ray, two of their favourite characters in the world. Ray the seagull was large and strong, bright white, except for grey wings. He was quite stout, with a longish yellow bill, yellow legs and webbed feet. The girls thought him terribly handsome.

'Happy Birthday, Bella and Ellie!' called Magic Joe as he slid off Ray's back and gave him an enormous hug and a pat. 'Thank you dear

chap,' he added to him. The two girls rushed up to Ray and patted and stroked his smooth neck enthusiastically. Ray looked very pleased with himself.

'How are you both?' asked Magic Joe. 'I hope well and happy! It's exactly a year since I last saw you. At least, that's a year in your time, but for me, well, it could be no amount of time at all! Thank you for coming to see me in my little home on the beach!'

'But Magic Joe, we had no choice!' exclaimed Bella. 'We got kidnapped here by an invisible giant hoover thing, and we haven't a clue what's going on, and we expect Mummy and Daddy will soon be wondering where we are. And well, while it's very lovely here, and we had a great swim in the lake... er... sea... er... river... now we're quite hungry and thirsty too!'

'Yes!' Ellie added 'but it really is great to see you again, Magic Joe. How are you, and how are our best Canada geese friends, Alberta and Nova?'

'Oh! They're really well, thank you Ellie!' replied Magic Joe and added, 'But, well now, children. Let's start by making you something to eat and drink, and we can sit down and I'll tell you everything.'

Magic Joe drew a flint out of his side bag and lit the fire. He took the kettle outside and dunking it in small wooden water bucket of rain water, half-filled it and brought it back to the fire, putting it onto a small four-legged trivet that he placed over the flames.

The girls sat at the table on the mossy tree stumps, looking on with curiosity. Ray the Seagull perched next to them watching the proceedings closely with his beady eyes.

'Now then,' said Magic Joe, 'how about some acorn cake?'

'Um, yes please, Magic Joe, we're starving!' said Bella uncertainly.

He rummaged about in his shoulder bag and brought out an old tin. Opening the tin, he pulled out four pieces of cake wrapped in leaves, which he placed on three pieces of bark on the table and added a few of the raspberries and a couple of hazelnuts to each plate. The other piece he put down on the floor for Ray, who started pecking at it greedily.

Bella and Ellie nibbled at the corners of their cake dubiously, until they realised it was absolutely delicious! Gooey and sticky, made with apricots, raisins, walnuts and along with the juicy sweet raspberries... they were soon gobbling it up. *'It must be magic cake*!' thought Ellie, as she ate it hungrily.

'Mmmm, delicious! Thank you!' they said in unison. Ray made a contented squawking noise.

Magic Joe went over to the kettle, and pulling some leaves from his shoulder bag, popped them into a tea pot from a shelf nearby. He poured the hot water over the top.

'Here we are then, girls – nettle tea!'

Bella and Ellie drank the tea from walnut shells (they needed lots of refills) and then, feeling relaxed and content, waited to hear what Magic Joe had to tell them.

Chapter 5

'Right well, I'm sorry to say, I have some bad news. To tell you the truth, I'm very, very worried about my twin sister, Magic Merry. You see, it seems that she has lost her magic powers and all her... well, merriness. When I call to see her, she won't see me; she won't talk to me and she won't answer even when I call our special 'hallooo' call.'

'Even her dear friends Hedgy the hedgehog and Nibbler the field mouse won't tell me what's going on. I have asked them what they think is the matter and they just say there's something bad, something nasty in the woods. But it's as if they don't dare tell me.'

'They say that Merry doesn't go out of her house ever,' continued Magic Joe. 'She has stopped feeding and caring for all the little birds and animals who live nearby, and she doesn't talk to anyone. I absolutely love my twin, and for all our long lives, I have never known her behave like this.'

Now, Bella and Ellie had not actually met Magic Merry when they had had that huge adventure a year ago. But they knew she was Magic Joe's twin sister. They had heard how she was so brave and merry and kind to the other four cousins when they were trying to save Ogo Pogo and had landed in Blaxhall woods. They had heard what a lovely, pretty and kind little pixie girl she was. And all about her very special tree house home. Bea, Bella's older sister, had often talked about Merry – about her special powers; how Merry had healed Bea's worried mind and anxiety that morning, so that she was happy once more.

'But Magic Joe, have you asked Merry's other animal friends?" asked Bella sensibly. 'Can they tell you what what's wrong with Merry? Perhaps she isn't feeling well? She might even be very ill?'

'Yes, I have tried to talk to the animals, and the trees as well,' replied Magic Joe. 'But they simply say that there's something bad happening in the woods, and are reluctant even to talk about it. For example, sometimes they will nod their heads if I ask them a question, but only slightly. They are not speaking much and not eating or flying or running about as usual. There is a sadness in the woods and it is uncommonly quiet. Rather a lot of the creatures have left to live in another forest a few miles away. I'm afraid to say that this behaviour has all the signs of bewitchment, a magical enchantment in the woods.'

Ellie started looking uncomfortable. She had been listening to all that was being said and was getting a funny feeling in her tummy, a feeling that lay somewhere between excitement and fear.

'But Magic Joe,' she gasped. 'What do you want US to do about it? We're only little. What can WE do? Why are we here, and in fact, WHERE are we exactly?'

Magic Joe smiled kindly at little Ellie.

'Well Ellie, you see, it's Midsummer days today and tomorrow, when earthly natural magic can be really strong. The sun is at its highest and nature is full of life, strength and growth. You two, on your birthdays, are full of extra good energy. Both you, and your brother Harry, Bella's sister Bea and your cousins Alex and Sophia have proved that you have special powers when you work together as a team. If we can harness those powers you might just be able to help. Today might be the only opportunity to try and find Merry and, if necessary, rescue her. I want to ask you, and only if you freely agree, whether you might be willing to come with me to the woods. I am planning to ask the others too.'

'And,' he added, 'as to where we are, Ellie, we are on a small beach on the river Alde at a place just near Little Japan.'

'Oooh, we know Little Japan!' laughed Bella. 'We sail there for family picnics and swimming, but this looks different, smaller, less muddy, and NO jumping sand fleas!'

'That's because I did some magic, and we are just a little way up river from there – we can easily get to Blaxhall woods from here.'

'But if we say we will help, how are you going to get the others?' asked Ellie. 'My brother Harry is staying at Parham with Alex.

'Yes, and my sister Bea is staying there too, with Sophia,' added Bella. 'And besides, won't my daddy Tom and mummy Dee Dee miss us?'

'I think you both know,' replied Magic Joe, 'that time has a different way of being counted when you are with me. Time will stand still in your garden at home and your parents won't even know you have gone. And as for your sister and cousins, well, they will find a way.'

Magic Joe winked at them, put his finger to the side of his nose in a gesture of secrecy, and gave them both a huge grin. He pulled a wooden stick with interesting carvings on it out of his shoulder bag. Bella and Ellie immediately recognised his magic wand and each gave a little gasp. They held their breaths.

He circled his wand three times in each direction and chanted:

'Creatures of waves, fishes of seas,
Come to us and help us please.
The time has come, renewed by sun,
To count our blessings one by one.'

Chapter 6

Meanwhile, a couple of miles away over at Parham, Sophia and Bea were just waking up. Bea, short for Beatrix, was Sophia's first cousin, older sister to Bella and elder daughter of Tom and Dee Dee. Sophia and Bea were both 8 years old. They had planned to have a 'midnight' feast and had got everything ready the night before. Their plan had been to wake up the two boys, Alex and Harry, in Alex's bunk room next door.

On that starry night, he four of them were to slip outside into the field behind the house, to eat their cheesy oatcakes and apples, and drink their chocolate-flavoured oat milk. It was to be a midsummer treat, to go out into the darkness and watch the light gradually change into twilight and then see the sun actually rise, about an hour later. But luckily for Sophia's parents Rose and Jon, the children had all overslept and the whole household had slumbered on until the morning.

'Oh no!' exclaimed Sophia sleepily as she looked at her bedside clock. 'Quick Bea! Look at the time – it's 7.00 a.m. We've overslept and missed our midnight feast!'

Bea sat bolt upright instantly. 'Oh bother!' she exclaimed.

The two girls threw off the bed covers and hastily pulled on some jeans and T shirts. Dashing next door, they shook Alex and Harry, the two cousins, to wake them up. But the boys in the top and bottom bunks were not to be woken. They yawned sleepily, turned over, and would not stir despite several proddings from the girls.

'Never mind, Soph!' whispered Bea. 'Let's go outside anyway.'

So, the two cousins ran noiselessly downstairs and grabbed the back-pack with the feast in it off the kitchen counter. They pulled on their trainers and shot through the kitchen door, through the garden gate, round past the green house, the potting shed and out onto the field.

It was a beautiful early morning. So sunny and warm, a low mist lying on the sparkling grass. Tinkerbell, the tortoiseshell family cat, was sitting on the garden gatepost cleaning her paws. She purred as the girls dashed past her. 'Morning Stinkers!' called Sophia as she sprinted past.

The field had sprouted into a beautiful meadow in the last few weeks. The grass was long and there were all kinds of wild flowers growing there now. Red poppies, blue cornflowers, cowslips, birds-foot trefoils, ox-eyed daisies and wild grasses. The flowers smelled delightful. Worker bees were busily buzzing about. It was such a wonderful morning, still and golden. It gave the girls so much joy and energy, they felt good to be alive. The two girls giggled as they skipped, jumped and ran along the narrow path that Jon had mown winding through the meadow. Two 8-year-old long-haired girls – Sophia's shiny auburn, and Bea's golden fair.

'Come on! Race you down to that oak tree at

'Race you!'

the bottom of the meadow!' shouted Sophia as she sprinted ahead.

It wasn't long before they both arrived there, panting. The birds were twittering in the branches of the old oak and around in the trees nearby and the sun was glorious. Golden and green morning rays played on the leaves and bark.

'But what's happened to the oak tree Sophia?' asked Bea. 'Look, its all surrounded in undergrowth, brambles and nettles – we can't get very close to it anymore.'

'I know!' replied Sophia glumly. 'It's such a shame, Mummy and Daddy haven't cleared all these brambles and nettles or the weeds growing around the tree for ages. Since last year even. I've asked them several times, and reminded them, but they are both SO busy all the time. I wish it looked different.'

'Could WE do it, Soph?' asked Bea. 'I know your mummy's got lots of gardening tools, cutting tools, rakes and stuff in the potting shed. Shall we have a go at clearing these weeds away, at least to make a pathway to the tree?'

Sophia thought hard for a moment – she knew how to unlock the potting shed, and she considered what they would need.

'That's a great idea Bea! Yes! Let's do it! And we'll borrow the old green and blue golf buggy that Daddy bought on E bay – he converted it to do errands round the garden. It's great - it has space at the back where mum puts compost and stuff to cart to the vegetable garden. It's in our hut at the moment - we can put the tools and stuff in the back of it to carry down here. That'll save carting them in a wheel barrow.'

Now strictly speaking, Sophia and Alex were never allowed to take the buggy and just drive it around any old time, without getting permission, especially from their father Jon. But Sophia was feeling rather carefree today, and thought that somehow, crazily, she wouldn't get into trouble. Who knows what gave her THAT idea! She also wanted to make it a really fun activity for Bea. She thought that Alex and Harry would appear anytime now to help out.

The two girls sprinted back up through the meadow and quietly unbolted the potting shed door. Sophia saw the tools hanging tidily from the walls on the designated hooks where her mother, Rose, always put them. They reached up and 'borrowed' a pair of snipping secateurs and some bypass secateurs – good for cutting thicker twigs and branches. They also took a rake.

Relocking the potting shed door, they stealthily crept to the hut where daddy Jon's buggy was kept. They placed tools in the back of it. Letting off the hand brake, the two cousins pushed the buggy to the top of the field. Tinkerbell the cat, pausing in her morning ablutions, froze midway with one leg straight up in the air. She watched them with suspicion, until, seeing the girls get in the buggy, she suddenly leapt down and scarpered away in the opposite direction at top speed, tail up the air.

Sophia turned the ignition key, and quickly the engine sprang into life. Bea jumped up beside her. The engine noise made Bea worry it would wake everyone up. But Sophia, foot on the accelerator, was soon hurtling rapidly along the path at the terrifying speed of 20 m.p.h., across the meadow, towards the oak tree.

'Woo-hoo!' shouted the cousins happily.

When they arrived, Sophia switched off the ignition, and pushed on the brake hard to lock the buggy. The girls sat there for a moment studying the tree carefully. Jumping out of the buggy, they circumnavigated the base of the tree, until they found what they thought would be the best place for them to cut back the undergrowth.

Grabbing the bypass secateurs, Bea bravely made a start on some of the thicker stems growing up around the tree base. Sophia took the snipping secateurs and attacked the bottoms of the nettles and brambles. Then Bea raked the cuttings away and created a clearing. Both of them worked hard while at the same time trying not to get stung or scratched. There were a few exclamations of 'Oi!', 'Ow!' and 'Ouch!' But soon they were getting somewhere.

'I say,' giggled Bea after a little while, 'I don't know about you, but I'm getting very hungry and thirsty. Can we have some of our 'midnight' feast now?'

Chapter 7

Bea and Sophia sat with their backs against the old Oak. The ground was still a bit prickly but cleared enough to have a reasonably comfortable seat. They spread out their midnight feast in front of them, leaving half of it in the backpack for the boys (should they finally decide to come out). Munching away at the oatcakes and drinking their milk, they felt comfortable and relaxed in the early sunshine. Leaning against the solid ancient tree reminded them of that time a year ago. There was a strange jolting of their memories.

'Soph,' said Bea. 'Do you remember last year; how dear Magic Joe had a beautiful carved magic wand and could do spells and stuff? Can you remember any of the spells he used?'

'Well yes,' replied Sophia. 'Of course, he was sensational! One of his spells made me whiz like a rocket back to the house with Harry – I've never run so fast! It was amazing! It was when we were here, quite close to where we're sitting right now. He had his wand in a shoulder bag. Do you remember, he circled it three times in each direction and said something about running through the trees so no-one sees.'

Bea added, 'I remember! It went like this:
Run! Run! Through the trees,
So fast, so quiet, no one sees!'

'Oh gosh! That's it!' exclaimed Sophia, adding, 'I wish we could do spells, don't you? I mean real ones that make something happen! Wouldn't that be awesome! Can you remember any of the other spells, Bea?'

'Well, I do remember a bit of another one,' replied Bea. 'It was the one that our lovely Magic Merry said in Blaxhall woods when it was time to fly home in the magic box.'

'Ooh, what did she say Bea? Please remind me!' urged Sophia.

Bea, remembering, said, 'It went something like this:

Earth below and sky above,
Fly away just like a dove.
The time has come, renewed by sun,
To count our blessings, one by one.'

'Oh! Wouldn't it be wonderful to see Magic Joe and Merry again! I wish we could! I'd especially like to see Magic Merry!' exclaimed Bea with feeling.

An intense look suddenly came onto Sophia's face. She looked at Bea and got up. Moving over to the edge of the tree trunk, she picked up two sturdy-looking freshly cut greenwood sticks, that had come from the tree. Using the secateurs, Sophia snipped off any side branches from them and sharpened the ends to a point. She handed one to Bea who nodded approvingly and stood up next to Sophia.

'Let's try,' Bea whispered. They slowly circled their pointed sticks in each direction three times and out loud they said:

'Earth below and sky above
Fly away just like a dove
The time has come, renewed by sun,
To count our blessings one by one.'

Absolutely nothing happened.

'Oi!' said Sophia, 'that doesn't really make sense, does it. I mean, how can we fly away just like doves? We haven't got the magic box! Anyway, the way we've said it, sounds like we want the earth and sky to fly away! We need to be much clearer. I think we need to change the words.'

'Yes,' giggled Bea, 'we haven't got wings either! And we haven't asked where we want to go. Maybe we need to say exactly what we want to do? We could ask to go and see Merry for instance, or Magic Joe, and that would be up to the magic to sort out HOW!'

'OK, what words shall we use?' Sophia said, and thought for a moment. 'How about: *Earth below and sky above, take us to Merry who we love. Open the way to see her this day, and...* er...'

'*...make it quick so we can play?*' laughed Bea.

'Yes, that will do! And then we have to add the bit about the time has come *etcetera*. Magic Joe always said that at the end,' added Sophia.

'OK, let's do it!' exclaimed Bea.

The two of them stood together holding hands.

Looking up at the beauty of the midsummer oak tree intensely, they circled the wands three times in each direction and summoning up every ounce of intention and concentration, repeated the magic spell out loud in unison:

'Earth below and sky above
Take us to Merry, who we love.
Open the way to see her this day,
Make it quick, so we can play!
The time has come, renewed by sun,
To count our blessings one by one.'

Chapter 8

There was a sharp crackling and snapping of twigs, coming from the undergrowth of the trees in the nearby woods. Nearer and nearer it came, along with the sound of trampling and blowing. Sophia and Bea shrieked and held their breaths as the noise soon seemed to be all around them. They grabbed each other's hands.

And then from the undergrowth, two beautiful fallow deer suddenly leapt out elegantly, landing surefooted. They came to a halt right before them. Tawny brown in colour, they had white spots on them, and a set of antlers each. They snorted a little through their nostrils.

'Oh my gosh, it's the spell, Sophia! Something's happening! Something's really happening! Look at the deer!' Bea whispered urgently.

Both the girls knew that deer are very timid creatures. Sophia had often seen them in these woods, but they were quiet and shy, and though they watched Sophia sometimes, they would slip away if she tried to approach them. She had tried to run after them once, but they were too fast and could jump hedges easily.

Bea automatically felt that she should bow before these two handsome creatures. She had heard that deer are considered keepers of forests, especially stags who are likened to royalty in the woodland animal hierarchy. Lowering her eyes and head, she curtsied slightly. Sophia, seeing Bea's lead, did the same.

The girls didn't want to frighten them away, but Sophia, feeling brave, and like Bea, being extraordinarily good with animals, said in a very gentle, coaxing and polite voice: 'Welcome deer, we are so honoured to meet you.'

One of the deer came towards Sophia and was within reach. This handsome creature with its majestic antlers looked at them and snorted slightly. But still neither Sophia nor Bea dared moved a muscle for fear of frightening them away.

'Cornibus' by Sophia (8)

And then the deer started to speak in a deep gruff voice.

'Children, my name is Cornibus. And this is my brother Aribus. We have come to you as requested by your magic spell. Your charm has opened a doorway into our world of nature, magic and sorcery. Your spell empowered us to come to you on this midsummer's day. We are mythical ancient creatures and we do not easily come to converse with humans.'

Sophia said gently, 'How do you do Cornibus and Aribus. We are very pleased to meet you. I am Sophia and this is my cousin Bea.'

Bea looked at the deer, perplexed.

'But Cornibus,' Bea said politely in a hushed voice. 'We are, of course, so pleased to meet you. But all we wanted was to see Magic Merry who lives in a forest at Blaxhall, not too far away. We didn't mean to cause you any trouble, and we certainly didn't think our spell would work. Not really, did we Sophia?'

Sophia shook her head in agreement.

'No, do not worry child,' replied Cornibus. 'The reason we have come to you is not just your spell. One with stronger magic than you also asked us to come to collect you for a reason greater than any of us. Magic Joe sent us an urgent message to come and find you if we could. Your friend Merry is in trouble and needs some help. The fact that you used her name in your spell gave strength to your purpose and intention to see her, and it called us to you.'

Sophia and Bea looked instantly worried – they were thinking about Magic Merry and how much they loved her. They wanted to know what was wrong and had all sorts of questions, but they dared not say anything else.

The other deer, Aribus, quietly came closer and put his nose to Bea's hand. She stroked his nose gently as if she was stroking the nose of a wild pony. It was so smooth and soft and she could feel his warm breath on her hand. She touched his antlers.

Aribus said in his deep voice, 'So now, children, shall we depart? There is some urgency.'

'What about Mummy and Daddy?' asked Sophia. 'Won't they worry about us, being gone? Oh! And Alex and Harry – they will wonder where we are!'

'In the world of magic, as I think you know already,' replied Aribus, 'time has no meaning. Don't worry, Sophia, when you come back here, if all goes well, it will be the same time as when you left – as if you had never been anywhere. Your brother Alex and cousin Harry have their own part to play in this. But their journey will be different from yours. Trust and allow. Now it is time to go. We must hurry – there is danger and peril lurking for Merry.'

Bea and Sophia gave each other a hesitant nod and then Bea, being used to riding ponies, climbed onto one of the tree stumps. Aribus trotted over and stood next to her. Giving a little jump, she swung her leg over and held onto a small patch of stubbly mane on his neck. Aribus felt very slim, lean and rather bony after the fat ponies she was used to riding. Riding bare-back was exiting, though!

Sophia, copying Bea, did the same thing, mounting onto the back of Cornibus. She, on the other hand, felt immediately unsteady!

Aribus started off immediately, gracefully leaping, swerving round and bounding over the obstacles in the woods. Bea leaned forwards as close to his neck as she could. She kept her head down to avoid getting twigs and branches in her hair or eyes. She felt amazed at the speed and nimbleness of his jumps. She was impressed that he didn't get his antlers tangled up in the trees. Then Aribus gave one giant leap into the meadow and galloped through the grasses at top speed.

Cornibus followed Aribus with Sophia clinging on for dear life. The last thing Sophia heard was Bea calling out, 'Hold on tight, Soph! Squeeze with your knees, so you don't fall off!'

Chapter 9

Around the time that Sophia and Bea were trying out their magic spells at the bottom of the meadow, 10-year-old Alex turned over in his bunk and yawned sleepily. Pulling his duvet up round his shoulders, he swiped at his ear. Something seemed to be pulling at his ear lobe. Very irritating!

Harry, aged 8, who was Ellie's brother and first cousin to Alex, Sophia, Bea and Bella, was half asleep. In his dreams he had the distinct impression that someone was calling his name. Subconsciously, he stuck his finger into his ear to block it up.

Alex then felt his nose being tweaked and distinctly heard the words, 'Wake up Alex!'

'Hey stoppit!' Alex grumbled.

Harry felt a sharp tugging at his blond hair. 'Oi... cut that out!' he mumbled sleepily.

And then simultaneously, the two cousins suddenly found they were wide awake, and sat bolt upright in their bunks.

'What the...?' said Alex. There sitting on the pillow next to him was Ogo Pogo. He was looking cross and impatient.

Alex hung over his bunk to the one below and yes, there, sitting on Harry's chest was Ege Pege.

'Oh my!' said Harry. 'We've got visitors.'

Two tiny elderly creatures were sitting on the bunks with the boys. Ogo Pogo (pronounced *Ohgo Pohgo*) and Ege Pege (pronounced *Eegee Peegee*) were two tiny elderly creatures about the size

'Oh my! We've got visitors.'

of Harry's little finger. With whirls of rather long white hair, they wore little pixie hats and had tiny upturned noses and bright green eyes the colour of the sea. Wearing small mustard-coloured sleeveless jerkins and dark green leggings, they had small bodies and skinny little arms and legs. On their feet they wore battered old shoes. They seemed to Alex and Harry to look even more ancient than a year ago.

'For goodness sake you two, are you awake now?' squawked Ege Pege. 'We've been trying to wake you up for ages.'

The two tiny identical pixie creatures lived in a matchbox on the windowsill in Alex's bedroom at the family home in Parham. Alex and Sophia's mother Rose, and her two brothers Tom and Joe, had grown up with Ogo Pogo and Ege Pege. Those two had got into all sorts of trouble and adventures even then.

Exactly a year ago at midsummer, Ogo Pogo had disappeared out of Alex' bedroom window in his Lego airplane. It was a near disaster. The cousins had to undertake a dangerous mission to rescue Ogo Pogo before he perished. It was an adventure involving Magic Joe and Magic Merry. An undertaking none of the cousins would ever forget. But that was another story.

Neither Alex nor Sophia had managed to see the two little brothers in their matchbox since. Every time they had looked in it, they weren't there. Alex had nearly given up hope of ever seeing them again.

Harry spoke. 'What's up, Ege? Why have you woken us up? Is something wrong?'

'You need to get up right away!' replied Ege Pege urgently, in his squawking little voice. 'There is something massively important you must do. You must hurry, get dressed and go and find your cousins Sophia and Bea who are already outside. There is great danger!'

Alex had already climbed down the ladder with Ogo Pogo perched on his shoulder. Alex didn't need any more telling. He had a distinct feeling in his tummy that something magical was happening. He recognised that lurching feeling from last year. Quickly he put on his jeans and an aertex shirt, while Ogo Pogo kept up a commentary, muttering, 'Hurry up, Alex, hurry up!'

Harry, throwing off the bedclothes, rummaged about on the floor and found his jeans, T-shirt and favourite football hoody. Pulling them on he asked, 'but where shall we go Ege? Where shall we look?'

Ege squeaked, 'Down to the old oak tree through the meadow boys, and hurry up! And oh! Don't forget US! We're coming too, you might need us. We'll go in the matchbox, Harry, and you can carry it in your pocket. Quickly!'

Harry grabbed the matchbox off the window sill and opening it, put it on the floor. Ogo Pogo and Ege Pege clambered in and lay down snuggly at opposite ends. Harry slid the match box shut and put it in his pocket.

Alex, hesitating for a second, ran over to his tool box. Rummaging about, he found the old but very useful Swiss army knife that his uncle Joe had given him a year ago. '*Can't go without this*,' he thought.

As they ran onto the upstairs landing, Alex glanced at Sophia's empty bedroom, her bed covers all awry. He gave a little shudder. He felt an enormous sense of pressure. Then the boys leapt down the stairs, two at a time, through the kitchen and straight out through the back door into the garden.

Rose and Jon slumbered peacefully on in their bed room, enjoying their Saturday morning lie in, blissfully unaware of the events unfolding outside.

Chapter 10

The two boys raced at top speed past the green house and potting shed and on down the winding path through the meadow towards the bottom of the field. They ran as fast as they could, both enjoying the speed that they could go.

Just as they were nearing the edge of the field with the oak tree in front of them, they saw a most extraordinary sight. Cutting right across their line of vision, jumped a large beautiful stag deer complete with antlers. As it leapt into the field from the woods they could see, riding on the back of it, looking poised and steady, was Bea.

'Whoa, Bea!' shouted Harry as loud as he could. 'STOP!'

But either Bea didn't hear, or she couldn't stop, or she didn't want to stop.

Next thing they knew there was another large handsome stag deer making the same leap into the meadow. This time the boys could clearly see Sophia hanging on for dear life, sliding half on and half off the deer as it continued galloping into the meadow. She was holding on with both arms round the deer's neck.

'Sophia!' yelled Alex. 'Wait! Where are you going?'

Sophia, seeing the boys running towards her, shouted back. 'Alex, you've got to help us save Magic Merry! We're going to Blaxhall woods! Help!' And Sophia's voice trailed off into the distance as the stag, with her clinging on, galloped nimbly past the boys towards the trees on the other side of the meadow.

The two boys had just reached the oak tree and came to a grinding halt.

'Now what, Alex?' gasped Harry getting his breath.

Alex looked around briefly at the scene in front of him, scratching his head in disbelief. Aghast, he observed his father's buggy, his mother's gardening tools, and the half-finished picnic. He was horrified. But he didn't hesitate.

'Quick Harry, get all the tools – and oh! Those two sharpened greenwood sticks there, they might be useful for something or other. Just chuck them all in the back – I'll get the picnic!'

It only took them a few seconds. They jumped into the buggy. Alex turned on the ignition and pressed the foot brake to release it. Within moments they had turned around and were chasing the stag with Sophia on it across the field.

The buggy hurtled along with Alex and Harry sticking to the path through the wild meadow as much as they could. Alex drove at top speed. There came a point, though, when the deer had swerved off the mown path. So, Alex simply followed. His sixth sense was telling him that this was not the time to worry about the meadow flowers (though he knew he might be in trouble for flattening them later).

Alex, who knew that the suspension on the buggy was broken, shouted, 'Harry hold on tight to the side of the buggy! Or you'll be thrown out by the uneven ground!' Harry was being jolted this way and that and kept muttering under his breath. '*Saints preserve us!*' he thought.

'Which way did they go into the wood beyond this meadow, Harry?' shouted Alex.

'Over that way to the right, Alex – a bit more – yes! That's it! Can you see the path through the trees?'

Harry, his eyes glued to the deer about 20 metres in front, could see its shadowy outline running into the woods. He knew that beyond the woods was a large pond, and beyond the pond, a hedge. He felt anxious about those. He started wondering where the deer were heading, and a dreadful suspicion came over him. Alex already had a terrible knowing sensation.

The boys ducked and dived as low branches seemed to want to grab them as they went past. The green woods were thick with leaf. It was hard to see.

'Alex, they went that way!' Harry yelled, squinting. 'Over there through to the other side of the trees, out that way. Quick!'

They emerged from the woods just in time to see the deer, with Sophia still clinging onto it, skirt round the edge of the pond and, giving an enormous leap, cleared the ditch and tall hedge beyond.

The buggy seemed to take on a will of its own. Swerving to avoid the deep pond it charged downhill straight for the ditch and the hedge on the other side of it.

Harry and Alex both screamed – 'Arghh!' – and shut their eyes tight. Lots of tiny muffled squeaky yells could be heard coming from Harry's pocket.

And then the most extraordinary and wonderful thing happened. The buggy did NOT ram down into the ditch, did NOT plough into the hedge OR come to a shuddering halt, as the boys had expected. Instead it took off and literally flew up and over the ditch, over the hedge and landed in the next field with a jolt, on all four wheels.

The boys opened their eyes. 'Awesome! Right-on!' they shouted, laughing with relief. Now, high pitched squeaky cheers came from Harry's hoody pocket. Alex put his foot down on the accelerator. They could just see the girls ahead riding at top speed – the chase was on!

Golf Buggy chase (2 cylinders). Top speed 20 mph. By Alex (10).

Chapter 11

Back at the enchanted beach, Bella and Ellie waited with baited breath to see what would happen after Magic Joe's spell. Two shiny smooth football shaped heads emerged from the water nearby. Blowing through their nostrils, two harbour seals made their way up onto the beach. They came quite quickly, their bodies moving like caterpillars. Using their little front paw flippers and forked-feet fish tails, they hauled their fat shiny bodies across the sand.

Each seal was slightly different. One was silver grey with a lighter grey belly, and the other was a light golden colour with spots and a paler belly. They had rounded heads and V shaped noses with long whiskers sticking out either side of their cheeks and along their eyebrows. They looked so smiley and happy with their chubby, kitten like faces. The girls couldn't actually see any ears until the seals were closer and then they saw little holes in the sides of their heads. But what struck the children were the seals' beautiful brown mournful shiny eyes. They were adorable.

'Ah, there you are my special friends!' cried Magic Joe, clapping his hands excitedly. 'Thank you both so much for coming to help us – we are really grateful, for we are in a hurry to get along now on this midsummer's day. We must do what we can to help Merry.'

'Bella and Ellie,' said Magic Joe, 'these are two of my dear river friends, the seal sisters. This

Saley and Galey, the seals.

beautiful silvery one is called Saley and this golden beauty is Galey. I have used my magic to call them to us and they have agreed to carry you up the river to the edge of Blaxhall woods. From there we will find another way. Are you ready?' Picking up the girls' little trainers, Magic Joe placed them in his seemingly bottomless shoulder bag.

Bella and Ellie, feeling startled, nodded their

heads vigorously while silently both wondering how on earth this would work out.

'Cripes! Seals... aren't they slippery? Do they bite?' thought Bella.

'Will it be safe without life jackets?' pondered Ellie.

But they didn't want to appear cowardly, so they just smiled sweetly.

The seals turned around and slithered back into the water, until it just lapped at their bellies. They smiled encouragingly at the little cousins and gave instructions with breathy barking voices: 'Climb on quickly. On! On!'

Bella and Ellie grabbed their hoodies and slipped them over their heads. They pulled up their leggings to over their knees. Then wobbling slightly, they climbed onto the seals' rather fat, slippery and warm backs. They felt smooth and rubbery. It was a bit like getting on one of those inflatable swimming pool tortoises, but without the sharp edges and less tippy.

Bella's seal was the silvery seal called Saley, and Ellie's was Galey the golden seal. Ray the seagull, as if on cue, landed next to Magic Joe, who jumped nimbly onto his back. Leaning forwards, the girls put their arms around the necks of their two seals, stroking and patting them.

'They're really nice, Ellie!' called Bella. And at that, Saley turned her head round and blew some raspberries from her whiskery snout at Bella, who laughed with joy. Bella, used to riding ponies with her sister Bea, found riding a seal pretty easy.

As they set off, she loved the sensation of going through the water so smoothly, but she was glad it was not windy and there were no real waves to speak of.

Bella was a couple of metres in front of Ellie and Magic Joe riding on Ray was dipping and soaring some way ahead of both of the girls.

Galey, with Ellie sitting astride, seemed to set off very rapidly across the water. Ellie suddenly got a case of the most terrible giggles. It struck her so funny and unlikely. It was also partly her nerves. She was loving it and terrified of it, all at the same time, and she found giggling was impossible to avoid.

Turning her head to Ellie, the seal said in her funny whoofing, barking voice, 'My dear, please could you try to keep still? You are making my blubber wobble about. Do try and stop now!' Ellie, with tears of laughter in her eyes, swallowed hard to gulp back her giggles.

The two shiny seals swam on out into the deeper part of the Alde and turned up river in a north westerly direction. The water was sparkling and clear, little shoals of fishes swam past the seals, but the seals did not stop to try and catch any. The tide was coming in up river, in the direction they were going. It was helpful, carrying them along. The seals swam very quickly and smoothly, using their flippers and forked tails to accelerate. As they went, Bella could clearly see Iken Church, far across the broad water channel, pass by on the other side. She gestured and pointed at it to Ellie. Ellie thought how peaceful and quiet it was here on this beautiful midsummer's day. She now realised how lovely it felt riding this magical creature, feeling the warm summer air around her and cool water beneath them. She wasn't a bit frightened any more.

The two seals, guided by Magic Joe on Ray, kept swimming, leaving Iken village on their left. They entered some narrower channels with mudflats, bulrushes with their bulbous brown heads, and reeds on either side. The beautiful reeds rustled, waved and sparkled in the light breeze and sunshine. The seals kept to the middle of the channel, in the deeper waters, going in single file.

Bella could see Snape Maltings ahead of them. She recognised the huge concert hall, the board walks and outbuildings. She had often come here for family outings by boat at high tide. Bella briefly wondered if anyone would be around at this time of day and would notice them. She wondered what on earth people would think. But as they passed the big old barge on the left, moored up near the bridge, she could see that all was quiet and peaceful.

The seals kept on going, under Snape bridge which the road goes over, and on up the river as it got narrower and more natural again. They came to a little fork in the river where the river Fromus splits from the river Alde. Overhead, Ray the seagull led the way. Magic Joe pointed in the direction of the left fork. They swam on.

The beautiful reeds, waved and sparkled in the bright sunshine

It wasn't very much further and then the two seals swam to a narrow part of the river and towards the right-hand bank just beyond some woods. They beached themselves on the bank and their passengers slithered down onto dry shingly land. Ray landed too. Magic Joe hugged and patted him and then came over to the seals and thanked them most profusely. Bella and Ellie also patted and stroked the necks of the slightly fishy smelling, shiny creatures and looked into their sad shiny brown eyes.

'Thank you so much, Saley' said Ellie. 'I really LOVED riding on you! I do hope I wasn't heavy for you.'

'Not at all! You are very welcome!' replied the seal gazing at Ellie kindly.

Then to the girl's amazement Magic Joe once more took his wand out of his shoulder bag and began to circle it slowly in each direction three times.

'*Oh-oh. Now what?!*' thought Bella.

Chapter 12

Before Magic Joe had a chance to start chanting his magic spell, there was an almighty sound of breaking branches, crashing and crunching coming from the trees just up river. Bella and Ellie heard a distinctive voice that they knew so well.

'Oi, watch out! Bea, where are you?! Ouch! Help! I'm being caught up in the branches! Oooh, Cornibus, slow down! I'm falling off!' Sure enough, it was Sophia.

Bella and Ellie started laughing, clapping their hands in excitement. 'Look at Sophia! She's riding on a... a... deer!' shouted Bella.

A beautiful fawn and spotted stag deer, complete with large antlers, bounded out from the trees. It galloped straight towards them, Sophia clinging on any old how. The deer, swerved at the last minute, stopped short, and, breathing hard, calmly put his head down to drink from the edge of the river. Sophia went hurtling over the top and landed with an enormous splash in the water.

'Oh, for goodness sake!' she exclaimed panting. She picked herself up, and wading out, patted Cornibus' neck. 'Well, I suppose I should thank you – but really!' Suddenly she looked around her, saw the assembled group all laughing and gave a gasp.

Bea emerged from the undergrowth of branches, up river. She looked elegantly poised, back straight, mounted contentedly on top of her cantering deer.

Then everyone was laughing, including Sophia. Bea slid down off and patted Aribus who put his head down and drank the river water. She did a double take at the sight of everyone staring at her in admiration.

'Magic Joe! It's wonderful to see you!' Sophia cried, rushing over and giving him rather a damp hug. Bea joined her and together they greeted him like the long-lost old friend that he was.

'Bella, are you okay?' asked Bea kindly and gave her sister a hug.

'I'm great thanks, Bea!' replied Bella. 'Ellie and I just got here with Magic Joe... We rode on the back of some seals. Mine is Saley – look! There they are! We got sucked down a tunnel into Magic Joe's house and went swimming too!'

Ellie added, 'It was great! Mine is called Galey. She's golden!'

Bea looked totally mystified.

But before anything else could be said or done, there was another shout, the sound of ripping branches and the noise of a motor engine coming from the woods.

Bella and Ellie looked anxious and held hands.

There, racing up the side of the river bank, came a rather dirty blue and green buggy. It was driven by a hot-looking Alex with a red-faced Harry sitting next to him.

'Look! There they are! Straight ahead!' shouted Harry.

'Wait for us, Bea!' shouted Alex. 'For crying out loud, wait... wait a minute... WHAT THE...!?'

And then the buggy came to a grinding halt on the shingle, followed by a moment of silence. Alex and Harry stood up in the buggy and looked at the group with amazement. There they saw Magic Joe, looking very pleased with himself, Bella, Ellie, two seals, Bea, Sophia, two deer and Ray the Seagull.

'Oh wow!' exclaimed Sophia forgetting all her scratches and bumps immediately. 'Awesome! It's Alex and Harry!' And she rushed over to Alex and gave him a big hug.

'Didn't you see us behind you, Soph?' said Alex. 'We've been trying to catch up with you for ages.'

'Sorry, couldn't exactly stop!' chuckled Sophia.

Harry got out of the buggy and ran over to his sister Ellie. 'Are you okay Ellie? Is everything alright?'

'Yes! I'm great thanks,' replied Ellie. 'I've been riding on a seal!'

'Oh... that's good!' replied Harry while privately thinking to himself '*That's bonkers*!'

Suddenly, from out of Harry's pocket came a squeaking squawking sound. 'Let us out! Let us out!' came two little voices.

Harry reached in his pocket and pulled out the matchbox. All the children held their breaths. Harry opened the box and two very small, dishevelled creatures sat up and rubbed their heads.

'Ooh, that was really bumpy!' squeaked Ege Pege shakily.

'Yes! You kept jabbing your knee into my back!' replied Ogo Pogo irritably.

'Welcome Ogo Pogo and Ege Pege,' said Magic Joe with a smile.

Sophia, Bea, Bella and Ellie crowded round the little matchbox in Harry's palm. They smiled and greeted the two tiny pixies with great enthusiasm, asking how they were and stroking their minute wrinkly little hands.

'Yes well, very well, thank you very much!' said Ogo Pogo feeling better immediately and smiling at Magic Joe.

'Now then everybody,' said Magic Joe assertively and seriously. 'It is absolutely excellent that we are all here together at last. We all need to sit down and have some refreshments. And we need to talk.'

Chapter 13

Everyone sat in a group by the sunny riverside, Ogo Pogo and Ege Pege elevated on a boulder. Sophia took off her jeans and trainers and laid them out to dry on the grass in the sunshine.

Alex retrieved what was left of the midnight feast from the back of the buggy, and spread out the cheesy oatcakes, the flask of oat milk and the cups on a rock. He handed round a bottle of water. Magic Joe, giving back Bella and Ellie's trainers, produced still more pieces of his seemingly endless supply of delicious gooey acorn cake. The two seals were seen in the river dipping and ducking their heads looking for fish. Ray the seagull pecked at some crumbs. The two deer, Cornibus and Aribus gently nibbled at the green grass near the water's edge. Everyone felt peaceful and content as they munched their food.

It was peaceful as they munched their food

Magic Joe looking at them all felt strangely apprehensive. Even he, with all his magic and years of experience had never thought anything could possibly go wrong with his twin sister. He cleared his throat and began.

'I expect you're all wondering why we are here and what this is all about. Well, to be honest, I'm not really sure. All I know is that something truly wicked is happening in those woods just over there. And I don't have the magic or the strength on my own to make it go away. I have tried.'

'Do you remember how exactly a year ago, children, the six of you used your special powers, your powers of intuition, your sixth senses, to help you find missing Ogo Pogo?' (Ogo Pogo looked a little sheepish at that). 'And I was called upon to be part of that mission in the end, and be able to give you a little helping hand. Though you did most of it completely on your own. Now I am in a situation where I need YOUR help. I need your special powers again.' Magic Joe paused, then asked, 'Have you all heard of a goblin?'

'Well I haven't actually,' replied Ellie truthfully. 'Is it something that gobbles things up?'

'Yes, in a way,' said Magic Joe. 'You see, we have all sorts of different types of magical woodland creatures living in amongst the trees. There are some which are really kind hearted, like faeries, elves and pixies. Sometimes you might see imps, brownies and leprechauns. Once I even came across some gnomes and dwarves. There are tree spirits called naiads and water spirits called dryads. In one forest I came across tree trolls – giants and giantesses that look like gnarled trees.'

'These magical woodland creatures are nearly all good hearted and kind. Some may be cheeky or play naughty pranks (like imps for instance), but are never cruel. In this way everyone lives together in harmony with the animals, plants, birds, and insects. Merry and I – well, we are really pixies, but unlike some pixies, we have learned many magical spells through the years and our aim is to do good and lend a hand, wherever we can. Merry, in particular, has learned about many healing plants in the forest. Our dear friends Ogo Pogo and Ege Pege are miniature, dwarf pixies – very rare these days.' Magic Joe gave them a wink.

'But goblins!' he continued, 'They are nasty, cruel creatures. Their main purpose is to cause trouble. Sometimes goblins travel in groups, but sometimes alone. They usually live in caves or dark places under trees. They are hideous, ugly and bad. They are sneaky and hide away, doing cruel things without being at all brave. They have been known to carry weapons. They are greedy and eat food intended for other animals, they steal and they hurt other creatures.'

'Goblins are about half a metre high – about the same height as myself and Merry. They often have red or yellow dull eyes. They have beaky noses on flat faces and their ears are very pointy. They have small mouths and large sharp brown and black fang-like teeth. Their skin colour is often green or even yellow. You can't mistake a goblin for anything else because they are just so ugly. One other thing, they have a strange and disgusting smell.'

'Ooh, I once saw a picture of a goblin in one of my fairy story books,' said Sophia. 'It was scary!'

'Yes, you're right Sophia,' continued Magic Joe. 'Hardly any creature dares even mention the word 'goblin' for fear of talking one up. However, I have been told by my scouts that there is a wicked goblin who has started living in Blaxhall forest just on the other side of this river. I am glad to say he is not a hobgoblin (they are even worse and much larger).'

'But this particular goblin has conjured up a black swirling cloud around him which gobbles up every little bit of goodness and positivity it can find. This wicked goblin's cloud spirals around the woods looking for 'food' to gobble up. This goblin's food is kindness, hopes, dreams, happiness, acts of bravery, magic, beauty, joy, energy and every good thought or motive that is in the creatures in the forest. 'Once it has sucked up all the good things, all that's left is just a growing mass of negative darkness.

'Any animal or plant, however large or small – whether it is a caterpillar or a deer, a fairy or a squirrel, is in danger. If it is caught inside this spiralling blackness, and is not strong enough to withstand it, it has all its goodness sucked out. That doesn't mean it turns bad – but it becomes a shadowy poorly creature that can't function in the normal way. It becomes weak, loses hope and stays only half alive. This goblin is a horrible and cruel creature. The animals I have spoken to have no understanding of how or why he is there. But they say that once he has destroyed the beauty and energy of those woods, he will move on to another and start again.'

Harry gave a low whistle and shivered.

'But Magic Joe,' asked Bea anxiously, 'why can't Merry just run away, like some of the other creatures are doing?'

'Well, I don't exactly know the answer to that question,' replied Magic Joe. 'I haven't been able to talk to her. I have a bad feeling that perhaps she has already been sucked out by the black cloud and is really unwell. In addition, I suspect, in any case, that she would not run away and just abandon her friends.'

Just then, as if on cue, a flock of sparrows flew amongst the group. They were twittering and calling out in their tiny agitated voices as they flew past. The children distinctly heard the words: 'Run! Run away! Stay away! It's too late! It's too late!' And then they were gone.

The children looked at each other and shuddered. Alex felt afraid. He was the eldest of the grandchildren and more than aware of the great responsibility he had for them all. He flinched inwardly, thinking, '*What do those birds mean, it's too late? Too late for what?*'

'Magic Joe,' he said unselfishly. 'Are you sure this is a good idea? After all, Ellie's only just about to be 5 and Bella only 6. It's their birthdays and

it would be terrible if they got hurt or something happened to them. Wouldn't it be better to leave those two little ones out of this and let the rest of us older ones try and help?'

'Yes, Magic Joe,' said Harry, 'If anything happened to my little sister, I would never be able to forgive myself.'

'Me neither,' added Bea. 'Can't they stay here and wait for us?'

Magic Joe looked at the cousins. 'Well, Alex, that's a very brave and good thought,' he replied, 'but Harry and Bea, the fact that it is Bella and

Ellie's birthdays AND midsummer makes it almost impossible not to ask them to help too. You see, there is just this one chance we have, and it's today. There is one thing that this goblin actually fears. He is a coward and is really frightened of the very thing he is trying to destroy; that is – goodness and strength, purpose and energy. A good human being has more power in these things than any animal creature in the forest. Your sisters have SO much of it right now. Everything about them is excitement, magic, beauty, happiness and new life. They have more special powers on their birthdays than they have at any other time.' I know we will need to protect Bella and Ellie, but we need to harness that power from each and every one of you, to vanquish the wicked goblin.'

Magic Joe hesitated for a second and then added, 'But Bella and Ellie, you have to WANT to help and we can only ask you. It's your decision and if you decide not to, then that is absolutely fine. You can wait for us here safely on this side of the river bank. Your good thoughts alone will be of great use to us all.'

Bella and Ellie looked at each other seriously and concentrated. Their thoughts passed between them. For a moment they hesitated, then they nodded to each other. 'We definitely want to help you all,' said Ellie strongly and loudly. 'We will do what we can.'

'Yes!' added Bella. 'We're not staying here on our own, we're coming with you!'

Harry and Bea looked less worried now, but

Alex still had an uncomfortable niggling sensation in his tummy.

Cornibus and Aribus stepped closer. Cornibus cleared his throat with a little cough: 'We would like to offer our assistance too, Magic Joe. We will also do what we can to help.'

'Me too,' squawked Ray.

'Yes, and don't you dare leave us behind!' the two little voices of Ogo and Ege squeaked together.

'Thank you, you are all brave and wonderful. Now, let me tell you all my plan.'

"Now, let me tell you all my plan," said Magic Joe.

Chapter 14

But before Magic Joe could say any more, a most peculiar thing started to happen. The two seals who had been sunning themselves on boulders on the edge of the river, listening to Magic Joe, started to make some strange calling noises. It was an unworldly singing sound.

The children looked at them curiously. Were they calling someone? But no! As they looked on, they saw with amazement that the slimy rubbery skins of the seals began to look rippled and puckered. Around their heads the slippery blubbery skin began to part and a different head began to emerge. The skin of the seals began to slither and slide off the body of the creature

Two girls emerged from the seal skins.

inside. And there, emerging from inside the two seal skins, a bit like a wet suit being peeled off, or a snake losing its skin, were the hair, heads, shoulders, bodies of two girls. They pushed the sealskins down to their feet. Then kicking the skins to one side, the girls slowly stood up.

Harry whispered, 'Holy mackerel – what the...?!'

The two girls, who were about the same age and size as the four older cousins, were wearing tunics. One was made of finest silver gossamer and the other was of fine cotton threaded with gold. They had long, glossy, auburn hair which fell in thick waves to their waists, and large, luminous, brown eyes. Around their necks and wrists were shell necklaces and seaweed bangles. Little moccasins covered their feet. They were magnificent – simply the most beautiful girls the children had ever seen.

Everyone gasped. 'Who are you?' Sophia asked in a small voice.

'We are Selkies,' said the strange girl wearing the silvery dress, in a low, musical and silky voice. 'We are seals that can shed our skin and take on human form. I am Saley and this is Galey. Once a year at midsummer we are able to change into human form just for the day. We have shed our skins to become human so that we can help you today. Our strength can be added to yours. We are strong and we are ready. But at sundown we will need to return to these skins and take on the form of seals again.'

Even Magic Joe looked surprised.

He stood up and bowed to the two selkies. 'Thank you, dear enchanted creatures, we are honoured to see you like this and more than grateful for your help.'

'Now, everyone,' continued Magic Joe, 'gather round and connect in a circle as best you can. Hold hands or touch the dear animal that is next to you. If you are holding a hand make sure your right hand is up and your left hand is down so that you both receive and give in the circle.'

Alex happened to be standing next to Saley. He shyly took her hand. Saley held her other hand out to Sophia who in turn placed hers on Cornibus' neck. Bea did the same between Cornibus and Aribus. Bella was on the other side - she reached out to Aribus' front flank, while also holding hands with Ellie. Magic Joe took Ellie's hand and, on the other side, Harry's. Harry had his hand on Ray's wing. Ogo Pogo and Ege Pege sat on Ray's back and Galey touched Ray's other wing and held Alex's hand too. 14 living creatures. The circle was closed.

Magic Joe spoke. 'When a circle is closed like this, there is special energy that can be generated around the group. Here's how it's done. Firstly, I want each and every one of you to think of something really positive. An experience, a memory, something you love to do, something you are looking forward to, or someone or something that you love. Now, secondly, I want you to enrich that memory, think about it for another 20 seconds at least.' He stopped talking for a while.

Everyone was thinking hard. Sophia was imagining she was cuddling Tinkerbell, the cat she adored. Alex was thinking about playing a new riff on his guitar. Harry was mentally kicking a football into the goal at his Saturday morning club. Bea thought about how much she loved Magic Merry and the kindness she had shown last year. Bella was thinking about her and Ellie's birthday lunch party today, and all the family being together, eating birthday cake. Ellie visualised painting with beautiful coloured paints on large white paper on her kitchen table at home. They felt happy and contented thinking about those things.

'Now,' continued Magic Joe, 'savour these thoughts as if you were eating something delicious and wanted it to last.' He paused again as the children mentally concentrated some more on their memories.

'And thirdly now,' ended Magic Joe, 'I want you to imagine you are absorbing these thoughts like you would really good food into your bellies. These thoughts are inside you for ever, feeding and nourishing you.'

'Next everyone, pass the feeling of that memory to the person next to you on your left – that's clockwise. Don't speak, just let the joy and happiness that you feel, pass through your hand and receive the feeling from whoever is next to you on the other side. This way we are making a good energy pass round the circle.'

Harry could feel a really tingling buzzy

sensation in his hands and it seemed to go through his body from one side to other, as well. It was a lovely warm and happy sensation. *'Jumping jacks! This is cool'* he thought. *'I bet professional footballers do stuff like this!'*

'Now, repeat this after me everyone...' And Magic Joe chanted in a powerful voice:

'Mother Nature of all life,
Fill this woodland place with light.
Share your beauty and radiant love,
With all that live below and above.
Please take away all creatures' pain,
Restore their health and happiness again.
The time has come, renewed by sun,
To count our blessings one by one.'

And the children, who somehow suddenly remembered this magic spell from a year ago, all chimed in. They said the chant three times over and the selkies Saley and Galey, the deer Cornibus and Aribus, Ogo Pogo, Ege Pege and Ray the Seagull, all in their various voices, joined in too.

'Now,' continued Magic Joe. 'This is my plan.'

And the children – still holding hands – at long last listened intently to Magic Joe's master plan.

Chapter 15

Once they had all understood the parts they were to play in Magic Joe's plan, the group set off. They found stepping stones a little further up river and forded the brook. Lying low under the shade of the bank, they surveyed the woods ahead of them.

Alex led the way. He had been nominated by Magic Joe to be the path finder. Running quickly, keeping low to the edge of the forest, he merged into the shadow of a tree and waited. Checking his back pocket, he felt for the Swiss army knife and felt reassured.

Next ran Sophia with her magic wand, snippers in her back pocket. She dashed to a tree trunk, keeping low and lined herself up to it near to Alex, signalling to him to stay low. Harry ran like the wind in his fastest football style. He dodged and swerved. In his pocket he was carrying Ogo Pogo and Ege Pege in their matchbox. For once, they were keeping very quiet.

Cornibus and Aribus elegantly leapt and bounded into the woods, near to the three children already there, staying close to the shadows of the trees. Bella, Ellie, Saley and Galey ran next. The two Selkies were swift and light footed. Bella and Ellie were running between them as fast as they could. The four of them ducked behind a small group of trees.

Bea came last with Magic Joe and Ray. Ray swooped low, ducking between the branches of the trees, staying close to everyone. In one hand Bea carried her wand and had the secateurs wedged in her back pocket.

Everyone peered into the darkness of the woods. It was strangely quiet and eerie. The leaves of the trees around the children seemed to have lost their usual colour; they were grey, brown or sometimes black. The grasses around the bases of the trees were white, or brown, shrivelled and withered. Nothing was green, nothing seemed alive. The flowers were drooping and colourless. As they all looked into the woods and their eyes adjusted, they could see that there was very little vegetation. And the worst thing was that there was absolutely no birdsong.

Everything was drooping and colourless. By Bea (8).

Alex gave a low whistle. This was the signal to move forward into the woods. The various children and creatures ran forward to the next group of trees. They moved stealthily and quietly, each keeping low and in the shadows of the trees. They were making their way into the centre of the forest. The woods were a mixture of trees, not just pine, but even with the various types of leaf canopy, there was no sunlight filtering through. It felt cold, too.

Bella started worrying she was going to see the horrible-sounding goblin at any moment, and was losing confidence quickly. But then she remembered what she had to do if she felt scared. She focused on that lovely excitement she had felt, thinking about the family birthday lunch today! She felt better.

The party, led by the pathfinder Alex, kept moving forwards in stages, a few at a time, all the while staying quiet and hidden in the shadowy treescape. All of a sudden, Alex stopped short. *'Hey I remember this place,'* he thought. *'There's the remains of the fireplace we made last year - Merry's tree house is just over there.'*

Alex, whistling his low whistle again, reached the base of Merry's tree house. A marvellous thing it had been last year, up at the top of the tree - a beautiful little house, complete with a pulley system with basket, and slide, outside seats and flowers in pots. But looking upwards now, it looked forlorn, empty and abandoned. No sign of life, no smoke coming from the chimney. Deadened leaves all around and black cobwebs everywhere. The rope pulley had broken and the wooden slide had fallen down.

Sophia was shocked and disheartened by the state of the woods. She felt a sense of despair and of being overwhelmed by the task ahead. '*How on earth are we supposed to put this right?*' she thought irritably. Then she imagined her beloved Tinkerbell, sitting on her knee purring and dribbling slightly. She felt better immediately.

Bea remembered that wonderful evening just there in the woods a year ago. The happy time with the little fire and picnic and Merry playing her flute came back to her and sustained her.

Ellie's heart was thumping. '*Suppose Merry's lying ill in there... or even worse... oh dear, supposing she's dead! Or... supposing that wicked goblin is in there?*' And then she remembered she had to think of her painting and paints, if she felt scared. She squeezed her eyes shut and concentrated. She thought about painting sunshine yellow on a piece of thick white paper on the big table at home, and felt better.

Harry was trying hard not to worry about Ellie. '*Saints alive, she's only five,*' he thought. But he focused his mind on his fantastic goal shoot. And with the memory of it, he felt better.

Alex was hoping he wouldn't get into huge trouble at the end of all this. He knew Magic Joe had given him, as the eldest, the responsibility of being the 'pathfinder' and he felt anxious again. But he quickly thought about his guitar. He imagined playing it in the kitchen at home, while Mum was cooking, and it soothed him.

Magic Joe, the children and animals circled the base of the tree and connected with one another as instructed before. Ogo Pogo and Ege Pege, released from the matchbox, sat on Ray's back. They closed the circle and concentrated. They were mentally protecting Bea and Sophia as the two girls started the climb up, getting their foot hold from one branch to the next. Being both so good at gymnastics at school, these two had been asked by Magic Joe to do the initial climb.

It was quite a long way up. Several times the tree branches seemed to be obscuring their view and limiting their progress. It was if the tree was trying to stop them from getting to the top. Bea, pulling out the secateurs from her pocket, used them to cut away any dead wood that was in the way. Sophia snipped away at the dead twigs that seemed to try and catch them.

Bea was thinking, *'I don't remember it being difficult to climb this tree last year. What's going on? It was easy then. Now it's really hard.'*

Although they were both so good at gym at school, things like rope climbing etcetera, they found this increasingly difficult. Their hearts were pounding as they climbed and they began to feel fearful. Sophia gritted her teeth, thinking all the while of Tinkerbell, her marvellous cat. Bea kept her sights on the tiny cabin and thought about the time that Merry had helped her last year. After a good deal of effort, at last they reached the little platform that was wrapped around the house and front door.

It looked forlorn. The plants around the front door had withered – the pretty flowering climber looked blackened and dead. There were cobwebs around the door, and no sound of any birds or creatures around.

They weren't sure whether to knock. But they didn't as they thought this might cause too much noise. So very quietly and gingerly Sophia turned the handle and gave the tiny door a shove.

'I don't remember it being difficult to climb this tree last year,' thought Bea.

Chapter 16

It was dark and gloomy in Merry's little living room. At first glance they could easily see that the place was deserted. The fireplace was full of cold soot and ashes. The small wooden tree stump table in the middle of the room was littered with half eaten bits of food – an old apple, some hazel nut shells. An overturned acorn cup had spilled some liquid and gone mouldy. A bunch of dead flowers wilted in a wooden cup. And worse – there were the remains of animal bones littering the floor.

It was quiet. Sophia and Bea, bending down, crept further inside. Bea was shocked and dismayed at the unkempt appearance of the little house which had been so neat and tidy and welcoming just a year ago. Then there had been shelves with interesting-looking natural objects stacked tidily along them; pine cones, beautiful feathers, colourful stones, shells, and small dishes made of bark or wood. Now there were just signs of devastation. Everything was disarrayed, the curtains tattered and cobwebs were hanging all over the place. The only living things in the house were spiders it seemed. The air was stale and old.

But the worst thing of all was the foul smell. It was overpowering and revolting. Sickly and disgusting, it made both the girls want to gag. They covered their noses and mouths with their hands.

'Oh Bea, quick, let's just check the bedroom and get out of here,' whispered Sophia urgently.

'Oh Soph! I don't know if I can,' quavered Bea, glancing at the bones on the floor and shuddering. 'Supposing she's in there... you know... really ill. Supposing Merry's... you know... dead already? Supposing that goblin is in there? I'm scared.'

'Listen to me, Bea, remember what we have to do. Hold my hand, shut your eyes. Focus on the 'thing', that 'thing' that made you happy before. Remember that all the others are down below thinking of us with good thoughts – we are supported. Remember they are relying on us.'

The two girls stood in that little room and held hands with their eyes firmly shut. Sophia thought about Tinkerbell her cat and feeling the vibration of her purring as she snuggled up on Sophia's lap.

Bea shut her eyes and thought about Merry. But then she started feeling tears welling up in her eyes. She squeezed the tears out and focused again. Merry, laughing and smiling, the tea party in the woods a year ago, the way she had soothed and comforted Bea. A warm feeling began to spread around her body. She squeezed Sophia's hand and took a breath.

'I'm alright again,' she whispered.

The two girls crept to the little door into the bedroom and once more Sophia turned the handle and pushed the door open.

The room had that same dark forlorn feeling about it. Desolate. Cobwebs everywhere. Spiders. The little bed was unmade. All the coverings looked tattered. The foul stench. But there! There! Lying in the centre of it were two little mounds.

'Oh NO!' choked Bea. Overcome with the stench, fear and horror, she rushed outside and was promptly sick.

Chapter 17

Bea, recovering went back in to join Sophia, 'Soph! Hedgy and Nibbler! Are they... are they...?'

Bea crept over to the bed and joined Sophia who was looking at the little hedgehog and field mouse. They had become friends with these two little creatures in the woods a year ago. Now they were curled up together on top of the covers, apparently dead. Hedgy was a little ball of spikes and Nibbler curled with his head buried in his paws.

They looked utterly spent, and grey. Nibbler had lost his sheen and half of Hedgy's prickles were missing. No life seemed to emanate from the two dear little creatures. Sophia leant over and touched Nibbler's head stroking it gently. She bent her ear down to his nose. She put her hand on his neck. She could feel a tiny flickering like a weak butterfly.

'He's got a small pulse!' she whispered to Bea. Then she felt around for Hedgy's neck. It was impossible to tell. His body was like a hard, spikey tennis ball.

'It's no good Bea! I don't know about Hedgy. What shall we do?'

The two creatures did not appear to have any swellings, no rashes, they didn't seem to have a temperature. But they looked deathly.

Sophia glanced around the room. Apart from the little truckle bed and bedside root stump with an empty acorn cup sitting on it, there were many bundles of dried flowers hanging from low uneven shelves. The bundles were neatly tied with bark labels covered with very tiny handwriting. In addition, there were oyster shells placed in a row sitting upright, with numbers written on them. She went over to have a closer look. She carefully picked up the bundles of dried flowers and sniffed. They smelled of her mother's flowers in her garden.

Then she picked up one of the sea shells. Inside the shell was an ointment. Sophia sniffed it and dabbed her little finger in it. It was oily, thick and smooth. It smelt a little of marigolds. It had written on the front: *Number 4*. And on the back were the words: *Calendula. for wounds and cuts.* Sophia had a look at another shell further back along the shelf. This one had the words *Number 5. Lavender. Calming, antiseptic, for sleep making.*

'Wow!' thought Sophia. 'These are all remedies for healing. Healing plant ointments. I bet Merry used these to help any sickly woodland creatures.'

'Bea, look over here!' she whispered. Bea came over and examined the contents of the shelves. Both the girls were thinking hard. They were wondering whether there was a remedy for a dying animal.

Sophia was thinking about her mother Rose, and how she would often give her brother Alex and herself a special remedy if they were distressed. And although it tasted perfectly disgusting, she did know it was made of flowers somehow, and how it would often make her feel much better. 'I wonder…' she thought.

Bea was remembering something called 'Arnica' ointment. Her mummy Dee Dee put that on her if she had bruises or bumps.

Bea and Sophia started to look carefully at the rest of the shells.

Number 1. Arnica daisy. For shock and bruises.

Number 2. Chamomile. For disinfecting.

Number 3. Comfrey. For dry skin and spots.

Number 6. Oak. For strength.

Number 7. Sweet Chestnut. For despair and fear.

'Look Soph! Here's one for despair and fear. That might help them,' said Bea.

'We could all do with a bit of that!' whispered Sophia.

Lifting the shell carefully off the low shelf, she carried it over to Hedgy and Nibbler who were continued to lie deathly still. Bea and Sophia took a little on each of their little fingers. Bea rubbed a little onto Nibbler's neck and, for good measure, under his nose so he could smell it. Sophia, finding a bald patch on Hedgy's poor, patchy back, rubbed a little onto it. They rubbed a little into their own necks for good measure.

Going back to the shelves, Bea picked up the little shell with 'Lavender' written on it and sniffed it. It was such a lovely aroma – such a joy compared to the foul stink invading Merry's house. She dabbed some ointment under her nose and rubbed a small dollop on Sophia's wrists, who sniffed them. Then she massaged some onto Nibbler's forehead and added some to the bald patch on Hedgy's back. They sat either side of the bed, and stroked the creatures. It is quite hard to stroke a hedgehog, but Sophia, concentrating, tried to think happy thoughts about Tinkerbell, while laying her hand on that curled up little ball of spikes.

Going back to the shelves, Sophia picked up the little shell with 'Oak' written on it. She fished out a good dollop and rubbed it on her forehead. Then, offering the little shell to Bea, she rubbed some more on Hedgy's bald patch and Nibblers paws.

They seemed to sit there for ages. They began to think nothing was going to change. They each separately began to think that they should go back down the tree soon.

'Look!' Bea whispered. At last something happened. A tiny sigh came from Nibbler. And dear Hedgy uncurled slightly.

Sophia rubbed some ointment on Hedgy's bald patch and Nibbler's paws

Chapter 18

Magic Joe looked anxiously up the old tree trunk to Merry's little house. He couldn't see anything. In fact, they were all peering upward, standing there for what seemed like ages. A while later, Alex and Harry sat down on the earth and drew circles despondently in the dirt. Cornibus and Aribus were restless, stomping the ground. They were all hoping against hope that the girls would suddenly reappear with a smiling Merry.

At last something seemed to be happening. A blue-jeaned leg emerged from the dead-looking foliage and branches up above. And then another. Sophia could be seen climbing down. After a little while she jumped from the last branch and stood in the middle of them. She looked pale and breathless.

'Magic Joe!' she panted. 'It's horrible up there. We found Nibbler and Hedgy lying on Merry's little bed, but they were nearly dead, the place is a terrible mess and literally full of spiders and cobwebs. But worst of all... there's absolutely no sign of Merry. And there's a truly revolting stench. We used some plant ointment stuff we found and put some on Hedgy and Nibbler and they seemed to revive - but only a tiny bit.'

'Where's Bea?' asked Bella, concerned.

'She's just staying up there while I came back down to report to you. We didn't want to leave the two little creatures alone,' replied Sophia.

'Good work, Sophia', said Magic Joe. He

thought quietly for a minute or two, eyeing up the children, with his head cocked on one side. There was a deathly hush.

Then he said, 'Here's what I think we should do next. Bella and Ellie, are you feeling brave?' The girls nodded uncertainly. 'I want to ask you two to go up to Merry's house with Saley and Galey. Would you be kind enough to give that house a good clean, sweep out the cobwebs and spiders, and tidy it up. Do anything you think would help to cheer it up for the two little patients. Could you make it look as homely as you can? I'm sure you will find brushes made from branches and a mop of dried moss up there. We need to try and create a welcoming clean nursing home in which Hedgy and Nibbler can recover. It's been a terrible time for them.'

Magic Joe continued, 'You two are going to be the nurses and Merry's tree house will be the little hospital. We don't know what other poorly animal patients we might find today. While you're there, please could you make sure Hedgy and Nibbler both have water to drink if they need it, and do keep using Merry's healing ointments.' Magic Joe produced a little wooden flask of water from his shoulder bag and Ellie put it in her hoody pocket.

'Saley and Galey, please will you help too. Could you carefully search around this area? If you find any more wounded animals, take them up to Bella and Ellie's hospital. Also, see if you can find some food that could be cooked or eaten, just a few nuts or berries would be a start. Maybe some wild herbs to make tea? See if you can find anything at all at all that we can feed our small patients on. Would that be alright for you?'

'It would be a pleasure, Magic Joe – we are glad to help,' said Saley in her low melodic voice.

'I've still got some raisins in my pocket that we could give them!' said Bella.

'Yes! And I've got some dried apricots!' smiled Ellie.

'Thank you!' replied Magic Joe, continuing, 'Ogo Pogo and Ege Pege, would you please go too to help Bella and Ellie with the cleaning of the house – they would love to have your company. Perhaps you could help get the fire lit.'

Ogo Pogo and Ege Pege nodded enthusiastically.

'One more thing. When you get up there, Bella, please would you ask Bea to come back down as quickly as she possibly can? We need her here.'

Saley and Galey went off to forage for food and search for sickly creatures. They moved nimbly and stealthily through the cold trees. Bella and Ellie, sturdy and brave, set off climbing up the tree, branch by branch. Bella took Ogo Pogo and Ege Pege in the matchbox in her pocket. It was quite a difficult climb, finding their footing and pulling up branch by branch. But the two small girls were determined. The cousins felt purposeful and glad that they had a job to do. They felt emboldened by having Ogo and Ege with them.

'It's certainly turning out to be a strange

birthday,' thought Bella with a smile, as she hauled herself up from branch to branch.

A little while later, Bea landed with a light jump down from the tree into the waiting group. She told the others that Hedgy and Nibbler had revived a little more. Nibbler had gasped out that Merry had been kidnapped two days ago by the wicked goblin. But Nibbler didn't know where she'd been taken.

Furthermore, Nibbler had told Bea that the goblin had been really cruel to Merry, tying her up in her tree house, and starving her. In tears, Nibbler had spluttered that the goblin had even thrown out the small creatures that Merry had been taking care of, taunting her. That was two days ago. Nibbler and Hedgy, who had been hiding during the raid, had both felt too stunned by the effects of the black cloud to follow. They thought they were at the end of their lives. Their strength had been sucked out by the goblin's enchantment. Nibbler had explained that Merry had been struggling with the negative force of the black cloud for many, many days. That she had been so brave, valiantly trying to help all the other creatures in the woods. That was until the goblin had attacked her tree house and brought the black cloud to it.

'Come on everyone, we need to find her quickly!' exclaimed Harry looking really worried. 'What can we do? Shall we spread out and search the woods? Shall we go in a group? How do we know where to look? These woods are vast!'

'Yes,' said Alex. 'It could take us ages to search the entire forest. And then we might get lost and not be able to find each other again.'

'Ooh, I don't like the idea of that!' exclaimed Bea.

Ray stepped up. 'Excuse me everyone, but haven't you forgotten that I can fly above and between these trees and have extremely good eyesight,' he croaked in his seagull voice. 'I can spot a potato chip from 20 metres up!' he added proudly.

'Yes', added Cornibus. 'And we are fast and can dodge amongst the trees as well as swerve and jump over obstacles.'

'And two of us could ride on you and Aribus!' added Bea.

Sophia winced and rolled her eyes.

'We've got our buggy!' exclaimed Alex. 'Perhaps we could search through the woods in that.'

Sophia looked exasperated. 'Oh, really Alex! that would make so much noise, the goblin would hear you coming in no time!'

'Yes, I know, Soph, but that might be good', replied Alex. 'I mean, supposing we could lure him out of wherever he is, by making some noise. Not round here, obviously, as we don't want him coming anywhere near Merry's tree house with Bella and Ellie in it. But if we went together, with the buggy as well, we could cover a lot of ground.

Harry interrupted, 'Look here you two, we can't use the buggy, it's on the other side of the river, and the tide was high. We can't exactly push it over those stepping stones we found. And we can't necessarily rely on it flying again can we?' But he faltered at that, glancing at Magic Joe's shoulder bag, wondering.

'Magic Joe, what SHALL we do?' asked Alex in a desperate voice.

Magic Joe urged everyone to sit down.

Chapter 19

'Here's the plan,' said Magic Joe. 'I don't want YOU to be the bait. That's far too dangerous. I'M going to be the one to lure the goblin out of hiding. He will be greedily pleased to catch ME. I reckon I will be a prize catch for him. I will go through the woods riding on the back of Ray, calling to Merry with our special *'Halloo!'* at the top of my voice. That goblin is bound to hear me and do his best to catch me in his black cloud. Then, I dare say he will take me to wherever he has got Merry. Generally, goblins live in caves or in holes in the ground, and we don't stand a chance of finding him without some sort of bait. Ray will help me, won't you Ray?'

Ray nodded, blinking his bright eyes.

Magic Joe looked at the children. 'We will fly low through the trees, and you will always be able to see us. I will need you all to keep up with us, so that you too know where the hiding place is, and if I am captured, you will be the rescue team.'

'Hang on a minute, Magic Joe,' muttered Sophia in consternation. 'Even Harry and I, fast runners as we are, can't possibly keep up with Ray in flight.'

'Well, that's where Cornibus and Aribus come in,' replied Magic Joe. 'You four are going to ride two up on their backs – that is if the kind deer agree to it.'

The two deer bent their antlers to the ground in agreement.

Sophia raised her eyes heavenwards. *'Blinking heck, not deer riding again!'* she thought.

'Cripes!' said Harry, secretly thinking that he ought to brush up on his non-existent riding skills one day.

'Yikes!' exclaimed Alex. 'Are you sure about this?'

'Don't worry – you'll be fine!' said Magic Joe, winking. 'What I want YOU four to do is shadow me. Hide and follow. Cornibus and Aribus, you must gallop like the wind, move in the shadows of the trees, jump all obstacles and stay close.'

'Oh NO!' thought Sophia.

'Did he say JUMP?' thought Alex.

While Harry thought, *'Good grief! It gets worse and worse!'*

'But whatever you do, you mustn't get caught,' continued Magic Joe. 'AND children, and deer, you mustn't for a minute get scared. If you feel the tiniest bit frightened you must stay together and help each other by reminding yourselves of the things that make you happy. You have a lot of special powers when you work for good together, and I'm relying on you. And above all don't worry about me. Remember that. Whatever happens.' He added, 'Sophia and Bea, use your wands now.'

Pulling his carved wooden wand out of his shoulder bag, he invited the girls to join him in making a spell. The three of them circled their wands in each direction three times and all of them, including the deer, repeated each line, saying:

'By the power within me,
By the power of three times three,
Negative energy, you may not stay,
I release you, be on your way.
Earth below and sky above,
Fill these woods of dark with love.
Midsummer sun, take the pain
So that we are all healed again.
The time has come, renewed by sun,
To count our blessings one by one.'

And the strangest thing happened – the deer seemed to grow slightly. Their antlers became stronger and larger, their backs straighter and longer. Now they were taller, they looked more solid, as well as proud and majestic. The children felt different too – renewed and refreshed. They looked at the deer and suddenly knew that they would be able to ride them and that they would be alright.

The girls climbed onto Aribus – Bea at the front and then Sophia behind – using a nearby tree stump as a mounting block. The boys followed suit getting up onto Cornibus' back. Alex was at the front, and magically, he suddenly felt confident and strong too. He seemed, somehow, to know how to ride. Harry, holding onto him from behind, felt the same. It was a weird feeling – they instinctively felt they must have done it before, but had no idea where or when. Sophia was surprised how comfortable she felt. And Bea... well, Bea was completely at home. The girls carried their wands.

Magic Joe jumped up onto Ray's back and, giving the signal, they were off!

'- the deer seemed to grow slightly. Their antlers became stronger and larger, their backs straighter and longer -'

Chapter 20

Even though it was such a wonderful sunny day everywhere else, the woods were dark and dreary. There was no life in them. The blackened tree trunks, the empty branches, the general gloom and the lack of birdsong, was depressing and bleak. It was chilly too.

Ray swooped and dived between the dark trees with his wide wingspan – his white feathers were easy to see. Magic Joe, riding on his back, began calling out to Merry. His voice echoed into the gloom. 'Halloo there! Halloo Merry!' he called distinctly in his loudest voice. 'It's me, Magic Joe!'

Cornibus, closely followed by Aribus, leapt and dodged round the tree trunks and branches. They stayed in the darkest areas, under tree canopies, amongst groups of trees, and about 20 metres behind Magic Joe. The two deer, with the boys and girls riding on top, were nimble and sure footed. They did not stumble. Sometimes they cantered, sometimes they trotted, sometimes they leapt, weaving their way forwards in between trunks. The boys lay as closely forwards as they could on Cornibus' back. The girls riding Aribus, Sophia holding on tightly to Bea's waist, did likewise. They stayed low and they didn't make a sound. Magic Joe was making all the noise and the others said nothing.

The journey went on and on like a bad dream. It was so still everywhere. It seemed endless. Everything looked the same and the children had no way of knowing which direction they were going, or how far. Magic Joe's calling, the riding, the darkness, the bare trees, the lack of light, went on and on. It was exhausting.

The children began to feel bone tired. They felt drained – they wanted to stop and lie down.

Bea whispered to Sophia, 'How long will we keep going, Soph? I feel really worn out.'

Sophia glanced at the boys just ahead – they were drooping with exhaustion too. She felt it herself. *'I wonder,'* she thought. *'I wonder if this is part of the enchantment. Perhaps we are being affected by that goblin's spell and that's why we feel so weary.'*

She whispered to Bea, 'Bea, hold your nerve. Think of Merry, think of her kindness and her laughter, think of that tea party with Hedgy and Nibbler, here in the woods a year ago. Concentrate!'

She called to Alex and Harry in a low voice – 'Boys, focus! Think your happy thoughts! Cornibus, Aribus, think of leaping in the meadow in the sunlight!'

And then just as everyone was trying hard to get their thoughts organised, something happened.

A spiralling black cloud appeared from nowhere. It emerged just in front of them and was chasing Magic Joe. It was dense and black and moved exactly like a swarm of bees or a murmuration of starlings. A thick mass of swirling darkness. It swarmed and spiralled closer and closer to Magic Joe and Ray. It was a dreadful sight to see that black cloud sweeping towards to them. Then simultaneously the children noticed the foul stench. A disgusting nauseating smell that made them gag. It seemed to come from the black cloud. It got up their noses and made their eyes water. It was a thick, soupy, sickening smell and they felt as if they couldn't breathe. Bea thought she might be sick again.

'Urggh, this is truly gruesome,' groaned Harry.

Cornibus and Aribus stopped moving forwards and hid quietly under the canopy of a large dark pine tree. They looked at the scene that was unfolding in front of them, all of them staring wide eyed with horror.

The black cloud swooped down and totally engulfed Magic Joe and Ray the seagull. It was as if they were swallowed up whole - they could no longer be seen. And there! There, standing beneath the black cloud was the most hideous looking creature the children had ever set eyes on.

There! There was the most hideous creature the children had ever set eyes on.

Chapter 21

About the same size as Magic Joe, covered in sickly yellowy-green, scaly wrinkly skin, his eyes were a piercing ruby red. Black tufts of hair stuck out of his head. On each side were huge pointed ears. His nose was just an enormous green beak and his big mouth had no lips but sharp brown and black fangs. But worst of all, he had huge hands and feet with elongated fingers and toes with curled claw nails. He was wearing a dirty muddy raggedy tunic and had a curved knife in his hand. He was screaming at Magic Joe in his hoarse, creepy cackle.

'Ah-ha! Now I've got you! I've got you at last, you miserable creature! I've been wanting to catch you for years! And now at last I've got you! You AND your horrible sister. Ah YES! AND a disgusting white bird creature! YES! Now I have all of you! Ha! Ha! Ha!'

And then the children saw something that made their blood freeze. The goblin had grabbed Magic Joe's marvellous shoulder bag, and was tipping it up all over the ground, stamping and jumping on the contents. He got the beautiful carved magic wand and, breaking it in two, hurled it into the bushes.

The children shuddered; they could feel their hearts beating rapidly in their chests. Sophia checked her pocket for the snippers and saw that Bea still had her secateurs. She and Bea automatically clutched their magic wands tighter.

Alex patted his Swiss army knife in his back pocket. Harry gripped on tightly to Alex.

Alex, who knew quite a bit about tools, looked at the goblin's knife curiously and thought to himself, *'Oh hell! That's no ordinary knife he's got – that thing's a cutlass, the sort pirates carry. Eugh, so dangerous!'*

'Holy horses, what can we do?' muttered Harry.

'Just watch and wait,' whispered Alex rapidly to the others. 'Hold our nerves.' Actually, Alex wasn't feeling the least bit brave; his heart was pounding and his mouth felt dry. But he continued. 'We need to see where he takes Magic Joe. Don't forget the goblin is a coward at heart. It was part of the plan to let him capture Magic Joe. He will want to be captured to see where Merry is, hopefully. Remember how strong we are together. AND that Magic Joe told us not to worry about him – no matter what. It does seem impossible, but that's our task.'

The other children were grateful for Alex's bravery. They felt stronger. Cornibus and Aribus nodded their antlers in agreement. They silently backed up a little into the darkness of the tree canopy.

The goblin, and the black cloud with Magic Joe and Ray somewhere in it, proceeded to swirl away through the trees at a distance.

Then the deer and children followed swiftly and silently behind, keeping well out of sight. They dodged and darted behind the trunks, keeping an even distance from the black cloud and the goblin. They found the foul smell almost the worst thing about him. Arggh – they felt so nauseous. But it made following easy – all they had to do was follow their noses!

The goblin and cloud edged further into the dense forest. Then suddenly they disappeared.

'Hey! Where've they gone?' whispered Bea.

'Not sure,' murmured Harry. 'But he can't be far away. Maybe there's a cave or a hole in the ground or something? Let's edge forward and see if we can get a bit nearer. But be careful, we don't want to be ambushed by him.'

The children dismounted, signalling the deer to stay put. Led by Alex, the children edged forwards, towards the last place they had seen the goblin and the black cloud. Taking it in stages, the children dodged behind trunks, bent double, trying not to stand on twigs that might crunch or crackle. Alex, using his low whistle, signalled for them to get down lower. So, the four of them lay down and wriggled forwards on their bellies using their elbows to propel them. They came to a tree trunk lying right in front of them on the ground. It was blocking their way. The four of them manoeuvred into position behind it, and gingerly peered over the top.

And there! There, straight ahead of them in the base of the fallen tree where the root had been pulled out of the ground, was a hole. A large gaping hole. And around it were spiders and cobwebs everywhere.

They ducked down behind the tree trunk again.

'They're in there! I'm sure of it,' whispered Bea. 'There's that disgusting stench again coming from it.'

'Yes, I think Bea's right,' said Sophia under her breath.

'Now what?' whispered Harry.

Chapter 22

The four of them squatted behind the tree trunk. They weren't the least bit sure what to do. They were thinking hard. It had gone quiet and there was no noise at all coming from the ground.

Sophia had been pondering. After a bit, she murmured, 'I wonder. Bea, you know all those spiders we saw at Merry's house, did you wonder why they were there?'

'Well, not really,' breathed Bea. 'I was too frightened. But there do seem to be an awful lot of them around and look! Loads crawling in to that hole right here. Ew… I'm not very keen on spiders, are you, Soph?'

'Well, they don't really hurt, do they? I find them in the bath sometimes at home,' replied Sophia in a low voice. 'I think Daddy is more scared of them than me!'

'Oh! I loathe them', whispered Alex. 'So creepy crawly.'

'Shh, hang on a minute everyone,' Harry murmured. 'I wonder…' Harry was thinking hard, trying to remember something. Then his eyes brightened. He said quietly, 'I read in a book once about Spider Man, that the guy… er… his name was Peter Parker… was bitten by a spider which gave him those supernatural powers. Some people think spiders are lucky, and if you have a spider's web in your house it's supposed to be REALLY lucky. Spiders must be pretty intelligent to weave webs the way they do. But for some reason we humans often just don't like the look of them.'

'No kidding!' muttered Alex.

Harry paused, then continued slowly, 'I'm just wondering if that beastly goblin is somehow using spiders to create that black cloud… perhaps the black cloud is not just a black cloud at all, but is actually made of a lot of webs all joined together a bit like a huge sticky net. If so, in some ways I feel a bit sorry for those spiders. Suppose they have been enchanted and are being used against their wills to help that goblin destroy everything that is brave and good?'

'Wow, Harry! That's an amazing thought!' agreed Sophia. 'I'd never thought about spiders in that way.'

'Well, I'm not sure how all that helps,' whispered Bea.' What do you have in mind, Harry?'

'I'm thinking that somehow, if that was the case, we could (not saying we can!) try to reverse the goblin's spider enchantment. That way the spiders could become our allies, not our enemies. We could try to get them to work with us, not against us.'

Alex suddenly looked up at them all. He somehow knew that what Harry was saying was the truth of the situation. 'Harry! You're a genius! I always knew it! You've actually got the solution!'

'But how, exactly?' muttered Sophia impatiently.

'By using your magic wands, Soph! We can reverse the spell using your magic wands!'

'What?' gasped Sophia. 'Do you mean those

magic wands that we made back at Parham? Those bits of stick from round the old oak tree, that Bea and I used as a pretend game? Are you joking?'

'No look, Alex that's simply unreal,' muttered Bea gloomily. 'We only conjured up Cornibus and Aribus because Magic Joe had wanted them to fetch us. I am sure we didn't do it all ourselves with our pathetic little spell.'

Just then, Harry made a dash for the open ground next to the tree trunk.

'What's he doing!? Stop Harry!' called the other three in hysterical whispers.

But Harry, in his best football dodging style, sprinted, swerved and jumped over the obstacles until he had reached the bushes where they last saw the goblin. Without any hesitation, he dived into the bushes and rummaged around for a few seconds. It didn't take him long to find what he was looking for. Without further ado he shot back to the tree trunk and, hurdling over it, squatted down beside the others, panting. In his hand were the two pieces of Magic Joe's broken wooden wand, slung into the bushes by the goblin. He handed one to Alex and held the other half himself.

'Oh crikey, Harry! That was SO brave!' whispered Bea admiringly. 'Awesome!' And Bea hugged him while Alex and Sophia patted Harry on the back. It reminded him of when he scored that goal on the soccer pitch. It was a great feeling and he seemed to feel even more confident now.

In fact, now that they had Magic Joe's magic wand, even if it was in two pieces, they all felt stronger.

'Right now! Let's hurry! It's time to make a spell!' Alex said under his breath.

'What's he doing?! STOP Harry!' Called the other three in hysterical whispers.

Chapter 23

Back at Merry's tree house, the two little cousins Bella and Ellie were getting on famously with creating an animal hospital. Setting about with purpose, they swept and dusted the appallingly messy little cabin. Using the brooms made from twigs and leaves, they managed to sweep most of the spiders and spiders' webs out of the house and out of the windows. They swept the floors and got rid of the decayed food and bones. They shooed the spiders off Merry's wrap-around deck too, so that they hung down from it in threads like decorative mobiles. They used the mops of moss to polish the table and dust the shelves. The furniture was put upright. Some lavender flowers from a bunch hanging in Merry's bedroom were rubbed and sprinkled into little wooden bowls on the living room table – things began to smell slightly better. Anything torn or broken was neatly stacked up in a pile outside the house. The children watered the dead looking plants on the veranda.

They swept and tidied the bedroom, shooing all the spiders out of there as well. They neatened up the shelves and folded the little mossy covers and leaf blankets that were strewn all over the room. They checked all the ointments and herbs and made a mental note of what was available.

Using Merry's flint, Ogo Pogo and Ege Pege managed (with much cursing and grumbling) to get the little fire in the grate going. Old dry twigs, bits

Bella swept the floor and Ellie used a sponge and a bucket of water. The fire was lit. By Bella (5).

of bark and pine cones burned nicely. Bella and Ellie found some rain water in a wooden container on the deck and using a little pan, put it on the grate to simmer.

Bella and Ellie repeatedly went to see Hedgy the hedgehog and Nibbler the field mouse in the bedroom. They rubbed the precious ointment onto their foreheads. They gave them lots of pats and strokes. Hedgy and Nibbler began to revive.

With Galey and Saley's help they repaired the pulley system, which was a woven flat basket on twine that Merry used to pull provisions up to the tree.

Galey and Saley had ventured away from the tree, and nimble-footed, swiftly found just a few plants growing on the edge of the woods. They gathered some wild mint, chamomile, and wild sage. They also found a hand full of elderflowers, some dandelion flowers and nettles. These were all good for making teas. Ogo Pogo and Ege Pege added some mint leaves to the pan of simmering water. Soon Bella and Ellie were giving sips of herb tea to Hedgy and Nibbler.

On another outing, the two selkies hoisted up a few hawthorn berries and leaves. Very healthy for eating, if stewed.

But they didn't forget that they were also on the lookout for sick animals. It wasn't long before they returned with a rabbit. A grey baby rabbit, just half alive, looking very poorly indeed. With a very weak pulse and hardly breathing. Galey and Saley hoisted the bunny up to Bella and Ellie in the pulley basket. Bella and Ellie were delighted. They brought the rabbit into the bedroom and put him on the bed with the other two patients and started tending to him. Bella fished out the last raisin from her pocket for him and Ellie dipped her little finger in some dandelion tea and held it to his mouth. He sucked slightly. They rubbed some of the white chestnut ointment on his forehead and Bella gently stroked him.

In what seemed like no time at all, another little creature was hoisted up by the selkie sisters. This time it was a frog. Ellie looked at the frog and thought how sad it looked. Very pale green, dry and wrinkled. She could see his little heart pulsating faintly through his chest. She felt really sorry for him. She bathed him with water and gave him a drink of nettle tea, rubbing a little oak ointment on his heart. She gently laid him on the bed with the other creatures.

Next, up came a grey squirrel. It had a bad cut on its hind leg which was bleeding. Apparently, Saley had found it trapped in a dead tree root. It was in poor shape, its tail drooping and its eyes closed. This little creature was hardly breathing. Bella and Ellie bathed the cut and dabbed some chamomile ointment on it. The cousins couldn't think what to use for a bandage. They were used to tying bandages at home on their toys. But this was quite different on such a small squirrel leg about the size of Bella's little finger. Ellie ripped the label off the inside of her T shirt and wrapped it around the leg, securing it with her pony tail band.

A small flock of seven fledgling chaffinches were hoisted up. The tiny birds were gasping, their beaks opening and shutting with exhaustion.

'Poor little things,' said the girls. They set to work and gave each of them some elderflower tea to drink. They moistened a ball of soft moss and gently bathed the birds in the lavender water made from flower heads. They rubbed a little of the white chestnut ointment on their hearts. The baby birds, with their orange cheeks and stripy wings, blinked their tiny eyes in gratitude.

And so it went on until the tree house hospital was beginning to bulge with more than 20 little animals to take care of. They included squirrels, mice, a mole, rabbits, a badger, birds, an owl and even a couple of weak bumble bees. It was a positive and purposeful atmosphere. The little creatures, so still and quiet in their sickness, were slowly reviving. Nibbler and Hedgy had vacated the bed and were lying still by the fire on a mossy rug, recuperating. Ellie had put the little frog in a bowl of tepid water on the deck outside. He looked much better.

The poorly little frog recovered in the animal hospital. By Ellie (4).

It seemed a magical thing that no matter how much water the children used, the small flask that Magic Joe had given them was never empty. Nor did the shells ever run out of ointment.

The beautiful, glossy-haired selkies, Galey and Saley, nimbly climbed up to the tree house and had a rest for a while. The children sat outside with them, sipping the sweet elderflower tea out of acorn cups. They needed lots of refills. Ogo and Ege perched on a little side stump table. Bella sat with the sickly grey rabbit on her lap, stroking him. The group nibbled at some beechnuts that the selkies had found in the woods.

The animal hospital was hard work; they were all tired and rather hungry. They were worried about the others and they wished everything wasn't so gloomy, dark and dead everywhere around them. It seemed that their little patients were reviving but there was still a sad atmosphere in the woods. Saley told them how it seemed that more and more sickly little animals were creeping out of their shadowy hiding places looking for help.

'We have to stay positive,' said Bella. 'Let's hold hands and think about our favourite things.'

And the six of them sat still and focused on the things that made them happy. A warm glow passed round between them through their hands. A vibration, a buzz. They began to feel better, more confident. They felt a connection with the other cousins, and sent them their love and positive thoughts to wherever they were and whatever they were doing.

Ellie had a good feeling. She could sense that wherever Harry was, he was safe. She herself, really was loving the work they were doing, helping the animals revive. It was satisfying and she felt useful and an important part of the group. She felt stronger.

They opened their eyes. To their astonishment they saw Ogo Pogo, clutching one of the shells, clambering into the matchbox which was lying open by the door.

'Sorry all of you, I'm needed elsewhere!' squawked Ogo Pogo in his high-pitched funny little voice. 'See you later!'

And with that, he slid the matchbox shut, and it took off with a little whoosh and disappeared into the woods.

'And with that, he slid the matchbox shut, and it took off with a little woosh and disappeared into the woods.' By Harry (8)

Chapter 24

Sophia, Bea, Alex and Harry crept cautiously forwards and climbed over the tree trunk. They could see the gaping hole into the ground straight ahead of them. It looked dark and foreboding and awfully large.

The two boys were clutching half of Magic Joe's wand each. Sophia and Bea had their greenwood wands. They surrounded the hole. Circling the wands three times in each direction, they pointed into it.

'NOW!' whispered Alex. Together in soft voices the children said these words:

'Spiders of this dear green wood,
Help us now to make all good.
We know you wish to live and thrive,
So come you spiders, run alive!
Let the spell that keeps you bound
Be destroyed, so you are found.
Goblin's spell, we command to CEASE,
Spiders, run away in peace!
Now is the time, renewed by sun,
To count our blessings one by one!'

And then, the four children determinedly crept into the tree root hole, saying the words of the spell over and over again in their heads.

It was fairly dark in the hole and quite deep. It went under the earth at an angle, and at first, it was just possible to see into the gloom. But as they proceeded down the sloping tunnel further into the ground, they began to be able to see less and less. Soon it was pitch black. It was terrifying being in such a dark tunnel and not being able to see anything. They stumbled along, feeling their way forwards with their feet along the soft uneven ground into the blackness. Occasionally they would trip over a knobbly root or hit their head on a hanging piece of tree root hanging into the tunnel. It was airless, humid and increasingly filled with that stench that they had so grown to detest.

They went in single file holding hands, groping their way forwards slowly. Alex and Sophia led the way followed by Harry and Bea. They tried to keep saying the spell in their heads, focusing on the things that made them happy. It was more difficult than ever to stay positive, as the tunnel lowered and narrowed. Worst of all they kept feeling sticky cobwebs and hanging spiders in their faces.

The children had to start crawling on all fours. They each repeatedly touched the foot of person in front of them just to reassure themselves they hadn't lost each other. It was slow progress. The tunnel twisted and turned and soon it became impossible to know which direction they had come from. All of them did their utmost to focus on their strong thoughts. But their minds became confused and forgetful as they went deeper and deeper underground. Perhaps they didn't realise that the wicked enchantment was really beginning to work on their minds.

Bea in particular began to lose confidence. She hated enclosed spaces and felt claustrophobic. She felt like crying and tears pricked her eyes.

'Oh! this is frightful, I do hope I don't faint or throw up again, I do SO wish I wasn't at the back. I'm terrified of being left behind. I feel as if I'm suffocating with that sickly smell,' she thought. *'How on earth are we supposed to stay positive in here?'* But then she suddenly remembered the line in the spell: *'Spiders of this dear greenwood, help us now to make all good.'* And she managed to hang onto that phrase repeating it over and over in her head.

Sophia was thinking about her beloved cat Tinkerbell, and how SHE at least, could see in the dark - *'I wish I was a cat,'* she thought, *'then this wouldn't trouble me one bit! But oh! This is horrid, I hate it, it's giving me the jitters and I'm shaking like a leaf! Eugh, I hate the feel of these cobwebs everywhere. And now I can't think of all the words to that silly spell we made up.'* She felt very irritable indeed. She felt like screaming. But then she remembered some words, and kept saying them over and over in her head - *'We know you want to live and thrive, so come you spiders - run alive!'*

Alex crawled along with his heart thumping, hoping against hope that he would be brave. He felt so anxious and his throat felt sore and dry. *'Ugh! this is like a bad dream,'* he thought, *'and we don't know for sure if the goblin and Magic Joe are even down this tunnel! Yuk! That goblin with his sharp pointy teeth and dangerous looking cutlass!'* And he shuddered. Then remembering he was supposed to keep going with the spell, he uttered the words; *'Goblin's spell, we command – cease! Spiders run away in peace!'*

Then Harry in his dear, sensible, reassuring voice whispered, 'Hey guys, it's getting higher again, and wider!'

The four of them stood up, brushing the dirt from their bruised and sore knee caps. As they did so, they could see that the tunnel was widening out and there, ahead of them, was a dim, cold light. Alex instructed them to stay back while he crept forwards to look. 'Keep saying that spell in your heads,' he reminded them. Soon he gave a signal for them to follow. The tunnel opened out into a large gloomy cavern. There was a cold greenish light inside. Peering around the corner into the half-light they gave gasp. It was full of gnawed bones, small skeletons, rotting food waste and dead animals.

And there, there, standing straight in front of them, barring their way, was the creature they most dreaded – the goblin. He had his back to them, standing proud with hands on hips, laughing his course, cackling laugh, taunting something that was above him. Then with a cold shock each of the children saw what it was. The goblin was looking up at a net which was hanging from the cave roof. Tied up inside, his sprawled wings caught up in the netting, was a very poorly looking white seagull. Lying in a bundle next to him was a really pale and sickly-looking Magic Joe, and beside him, their beloved Magic Merry, who looked all but dead.

The four children's hair nearly stood on end, as the goblin turned.

Chapter 25

He was baring his sharp blackened fangs in the most frightful grimace. He was even more ugly close up than they could have possibly imagined. Muscly and strong, with his greenish scaly skin, his red eyes, his thin greasy black hair, his torn brown tunic – everything about him was repulsive. The smell coming from him was toxic.

But the children had two advantages. Firstly, that each one of them was taller and bigger than him. And secondly, that they had surprised him. He was certainly not expecting them.

Alex, quickly taking in the scene, noticed immediately that he was not carrying his cutlass. It was lying on a rock nearby. Bea saw it too.

The children moved forwards towards the goblin. Now they were chanting the spell aloud in unison. They got louder and louder as they approached him. It seemed to be infuriating him. The goblin stamped his foot, screaming at them to stop. They pointed their wands at him and, holding hands, kept chanting.

Alex stepped forwards with his wand pointing at the goblin. 'Let your prisoners go!' he shouted. 'By the power of the magic of these woods this midsummer day, I order you, LET THEM GO!'

The goblin screamed, foaming at the mouth, and shouting gibberish, jumped up and down with rage.

At this point, Bea, who was at the end of the line of children, did a very brave thing. She made a dash for the cutlass on the rock behind the goblin.

He caught sight of her from the corner of his eye, turned and lunged after her. Alex ran forward and grabbed the revolting creature from the back. He managed to get hold of him and wrestled with the goblin to stop him getting Bea, who managed to pick the cutlass up. She jumped over to where the net was hanging and, climbing up the side of a rock, started hacking at the black webbing. Close up she could see it was made of spiders' webs. Black spiders were everywhere. Out loud she kept chanting the spell. She felt a power begin to surge through her.

Then things moved very fast. Harry, leapt over to Bea, and pulled her secateurs from her back pocket. He climbed onto the nearest rock to the net and started cutting into the netting too.

Alex ran forwards and grabbed the revolting creature from behind. By Alex (10).

Next, they were joined by Sophia, who leapt up and snipped rapidly at it with her snippers. All three of them kept chanting. A sticky hole began to emerge and the net began to loosen at the top.

It seemed an unlikely thing, but Alex began to feel as if the goblin was losing his power. As he wrestled the creature from behind, Alex had the crook of one arm under the goblin's horrible green chin, pulling his head backwards. With the other, he held the goblin in a half-Nelson. Alex kept shouting the spell into the goblin's ear. The goblin seemed to weaken the more he said it.

Then the thing that the children had most hoped for happened. The spiders seemed to lose interest in anything to do with the cave, the prisoners or the net. They began running, running towards the goblin. First there were just a few, then there were more and more of them, ten, twenty, then hundreds. Alex stood back and watched as the spiders ran up and all over the goblin. His arms were flailing about wildly, as he tried to brush them off. 'Eugh! Argh!' he yelled.

And as the spiders crawled all over him, they wove a thick, black web. He was trying to fight them off, but he might as well have been trying to fight through treacle, for all the good it did. The spiders worked so quickly that in no time the goblin was cocooned, imprisoned. He could do nothing but stand there encased from neck to ankle in black. He looked weak, small, feeble and furious.

As soon as they had finished, the hundreds of spiders started running, from every direction, towards the entrance of the cave, back up the tunnel and out into the woods. They were running away.

Just at that exact moment, a matchbox whizzed past the group and landed with a little bump near the fire. It slid open and out came a tiny pixie creature carrying a silver shell.

'I've come, Magic Joe! I'm here!' squawked Ogo Pogo, his emerald green eyes flashing, his tiny voice squeaking, **'I've come to save the day!'**

'I'm here!' Shouted Ogo Pogo, his emerald green eyes flashing. He suddenly looked like the young little pixie boy he once was.

The prisoners had tumbled from the net to the ground of the cave. Magic Joe, with his eyes shut, was breathing hard. Very little colour in his cheeks, he was pale and glistening with sweat. Magic Merry was unconscious. Her clothes were all torn, she was thin, white and cold, and it was impossible to know if she was dead or alive. There was no sign of movement from Ray. The three of them looked empty, sucked out of all energy and life. They were like empty shells.

Ogo Pogo ran up to Magic Joe and rubbed a tiny quantity of ointment on his forehead.

Magic Joe began to revive slightly. 'Thank you, dear Ogo, for responding so quickly to my thought message,' he muttered.

Bea and Harry squatted down next to Ray and Merry. Bea was in tears. Harry had his arm around Bea and was talking soothingly to Merry. Bea was trying to feel for a pulse in Merry's neck.

Ogo Pogo ran over to Magic Merry. He dabbed some ointment on her forehead. Then he put some on Ray's white breast.

Alex was standing over the goblin, holding his Swiss army knife tightly in one hand. He had the sharpest knife in it opened outwards, pointed at the goblin's heart. Sophia, supporting Alex, stood beside her brother. Their two wands pointed at the goblin. The two of them were still muttering the spell under their breaths. They didn't trust that evil creature. Not one bit.

'Stay strong, Bea,' murmured Magic Joe

weakly. 'Everything's going to be alright now. You children have done well. Yes indeed, very well.' And he eyed up the goblin.

Chapter 26

It was a strangely forlorn and slow-moving procession that picked its way through the gloomy woods back to Merry's tree house.

First came Aribus carrying Merry, who was seated on his back but was lying forwards draped on his neck, still unconscious. Bea, with her hand on Merry, was walking next to them. She had carried Merry in her arms, like a toddler, all the way from the cave and up the tunnels to the woods above. It was no mean feat, especially when the tunnel had become so narrow and low. Bea was doing all she could to send thoughts of love and wellbeing to Merry as they walked slowly along.

Next came Sophia walking beside Cornibus. Magic Joe had managed to stagger out of the mouth of the tunnel and climb unsteadily onto the deer's back. Then Magic Joe had partially collapsed forwards with his little arms around Cornibus' neck. Sophia sweetly kept whispering words of encouragement to them. 'It's not far now, Magic Joe. You'll be alright. Well done, Cornibus.'

Ogo Pogo's head could be seen poking out of the top of Magic Joe's shoulder bag which Sophia had slung over her shoulder. She had rescued it and the contents from the ground where it had been stamped on by the goblin.

Following them came Alex leading the goblin on a belt. Alex had taken the goblin's leather belt off his tunic and using the buckle had tied it to one of the goblin's ankles. Alex was feeling strong and determined not to let the goblin escape. In one hand he carried his half of Magic Joe's wand and kept pointing it at the goblin to keep him moving. Alex also carried the cutlass. The goblin shuffled along, head drooping, in silence.

Harry, with the other half of Magic Joe's wand, walked on the other side of the goblin. In his arms Harry was cradling Ray who was lying there, breathing but shuddering periodically with shock.

It was a sombre and exhausted little group.

'We're all tired and hungry; Magic Merry is in bad shape, Magic Joe looks wrecked, and as for Ray...,' thought Harry. *'But thank goodness, at least we're all alive! AND we've captured the wicked goblin.'*

Back at the animal hospital tree house, Bella and Ellie were still busy with caring for the animals, who were lined up on the bed. The cousins were still busily giving them drinks and keeping them warm and safe.

All of a sudden Ellie stood stock still and listened. She could hear a bird. A lone bird chirruping cheerfully somewhere not far away in a nearby tree. Her ears pricked up. It was a sound she had not heard since the morning and certainly not one she had heard deep in the forest here.

Bella noticed something too. A few spiders which had been hanging about in the bedroom suddenly all got up and ran at top speed through the open doorway. The girls crept outside and, full of curiosity, looked about.

'Something's happening,' thought Bella.

Then they noticed something else. The spider web threads that had been hanging from the tree house began to glisten with drops, like dew drops, silver and gold. It was as if they were coming alive. The two cousins held their breaths while they watched.

'Something's happening!' thought Bella.

Chapter 27

The spiders were all running away from the tree house and into the tree itself, around the tree, all over it in fact. It was a hive of activity. Hundreds of spiders running everywhere in every direction, into every nook and cranny onto every branch, along every twig and every dried-up wizened leaf. They were covering it. It was like watching a swarm of ants busily running around, but these weren't ants, they were spiders. And then Ellie noticed something amazing. Wherever the spiders went, little tiny splodges of colour came back to the tree. It was as if she had her favourite paintbrush loaded with all the colours of every season of a tree, and was flicking it at the tree. And the flicks of paints started growing and spreading. The blobs of colour joined up and became one. Colour was flooding back into the tree; the tree was coming to life.

'Look Bella!' she cried. All around them the spiders kept running and climbing up and down the trees close by. Then the spiders took off around the ground of the tree, up and down the nearby trees, in and out of everything. The woodland was literally alive with thousands of little spiders running in every direction.

As the spiders did so, gradually the whole woodland around them began to fill with life. Little by little, birds started calling to one another. Firstly, the rich and mellow sound of a single blackbird singing from a nearby branch. Then a couple of great tits could be heard with their '*t-cher, t-cher, t-cher*' chatter. A sudden loud burst of song signalled that a jenny wren was nearby. A cuckoo could be heard: '*cuckoo, cuckoo, cuckoo*!' Best of all, the baby chaffinches, that the girls had nursed, suddenly flew in a little flock, out of the tree house hospital door and landed in the branches of the tree: '*Diddieoo, diddieoo, thank you, thank you!*' they sang. At last came the high-pitched whistling of the yellow hammers with their funny calls '*a little bit of bread and no che-ese, a little bit of bread and no che-ese!*' Soon there was the riotous sound of glorious bird song and the sight of many bright birds darting amongst the trees.

A warm gentle breeze caressed the woodland. Slanting shafts of sunlight started penetrating the canopy of the trees. Butterflies fluttered by. Bees started buzzing busily. Flies, wasps, ants, beetles went about their business. The woodland glades were filling with yellow, gold and green dappled colours. As the cousins looked down, more and more spiders appeared, running in every direction, every which way. Everything they touched, every blade of grass, every flower and plant they ran over, burst into life full of vibrant colour. Clumps of vibrant pink Herb Robert appeared at the base of their tree. Golden and apricot honeysuckle sprang up, twining through the branches, wafting its sweet scent around them. Bright yellow delicious coconut-smelling flowers opened on branches of gorse. Best of all were the dog roses

– delicate, scrambling beauties adorning the hedgerows with their pretty, pale pink flowers.

'Something really fantastic has happened!' cried Bella clapping her hands.

Galey and Saley climbed up to the tree house and joined the girls on the deck outside. The four of them surveyed the scene below with gratitude, joy and relief. Hugging each other, they stared in awe at the beauty that was unfolding around them.

'Oh wow!' cried Bella. 'Do you notice something else? That smell, that repulsive smell has gone! It's just the scent of flowers now. Isn't it?'

'Oh yes! That's all I can smell too! Oh! Thank goodness, what a relief!' replied Ellie beaming from ear to ear.

They stared at the beauty that was unfolding before them.

Chapter 28

As the others in the procession moved along through the forest, the older children also watched with awe the amazing rebirth of the woods as the enchantment faded. The four children, together with Ogo, the deer, Magic Joe, Merry and even Ray, began to revive. Their spirits lightened. A little colour started coming back into Merry's cheeks and she gave a sigh as she lay over Aribus' neck. 'Thank you,' she sighed.

The procession arrived back at the tree house. Bella and Ellie, Galey and Saley gave a cry of joy as they watched. They could see the goblin imprisoned in the spider webs, being escorted by Alex and Harry. They could see Magic Joe riding painfully along on Cornibus with Sophia at his side. Best of all, there was Merry, lying still along Aribus' back, but alive!

Saley and Galey let down the pulley basket. Bea and Sophia gently lifted Merry into it and Harry placed Ray next to her. They were hoisted up to the little tree house hospital and were laid gently on Merry's bed. Bella and Ellie set to work with the ointments and herb teas. They calmed and comforted Merry and Ray while applying the salves and administering the teas. A dab of each and every salve was applied to Merry's forehead, arms, legs and feet. The girls stroked her little cold hands to warm them up. They wrapped her in a moss blanket. She looked at them with deep gratitude. Ray began to revive with a drink of mint tea and some sweet chestnut salve. They spoke lovingly to Ray and told him how brave he was.

Magic Joe curled up on a woven rug on the hearth by the cheerful fire to recover. Galey and Saley gave him some chamomile tea, a spoonful of the hawthorn berry jam, and rubbed some oak ointment onto his forehead. It wasn't long before he began to revive and sat up.

Sophia climbed nimbly up the branches of the tree with Magic Joe's shoulder bag and gave it to him. Ogo Pogo jumped out and, taking his matchbox, went to sit next to him and his little brother Ege.

Ege Pege was very relieved to know Ogo was safe. 'Well done, you!' he exclaimed.

'I'm sorry I had to go alone,' said Ogo. 'But there really wasn't room for the two of us AND that ointment shell in the matchbox.'

Sophia also gave Magic Joe the two halves of his broken magic wand.

'Will you be able to fix it, Magic Joe?' she asked.

'I can certainly try,' he replied with a wink. 'Now dear Sophia, please will you ask the others to come up here too. Please request that Alex and Harry tie the goblin to the base of the tree and kindly ask Cornibus and Aribus to keep an eye on him.

Sophia swung down the branches and gave the instructions to the others. It wasn't long before the four of them were all up in the little tree house. Bea hugged Bella, Harry clasped Ellie to him and gave her a big smile.

'Good grief Ellie! This is like a proper little hospital! This is awesome!' exclaimed Harry admiringly as he looked at all the little creatures everywhere.

'Wow! You've totally transformed it!' exclaimed Bea. 'Look Sophia, look how neat, clean and welcoming Bella and Ellie have made it! Completely different from how it was when we found it!'

'We've helped SO many patients!' said Bella proudly. 'Ellie and me, Galey and Saley too!' We've helped to cure Hedgy and Nibbler, rabbits, birds, squirrels, mice, all sorts really. It was really fun. The magic ointment simply never seemed to run out no matter how often we used it. It was such a good time helping the animals, we loved it! Ogo and Ege were great too – they got the fire going!'

'I even nursed a frog!' exclaimed Ellie proudly.

At which point Bea got the giggles. She couldn't help it! She didn't mean to laugh, but she suddenly thought how tricky that must have been to nurse a frog. And it was infectious, and it was a relief. Everyone suddenly saw the funny side of it, including Ellie. Soon all of the children were laughing so much that tears were pouring out of their eyes and their sides were aching. Even Ogo Pogo and Ege Pege were giggling in their high pitched little squealing laugh. And Magic Joe was smiling his broad happy smile.

Chapter 29

Magic Joe took up half of his wand and, circling it three times in each direction, said a short spell under his breath. Almost immediately the other half of the wand flew over and joined onto it. His beautiful carved wand was back to its old self.

Then, without further ado, Magic Joe conjured up a large wooden bowl of steaming water on the far end of the deck. Alex and the others, including Ogo Pogo and Ege Pege, were instructed by Magic Joe to go and wash their hands. Alex, who had been longing to do that for ages (after wrestling with that stinking goblin), splashed his face for good measure in the clean lavender-smelling water. They felt so refreshed.

Shortly afterwards, three ravens swooped out of nowhere. From their beaks hung small string nets containing wrapped parcels. The ravens deposited the parcels on the table and then swooped away, cawing. Magic Joe unwrapped the parcels. To the astonishment of the children, there appeared before them a spread of all the most delicious looking food they had seen all day. Magic Joe laid it out on the little tree stump table on the deck. There was nutty acorn bread with hazelnut butter, raw celery, carrots, raspberries, dried mulberries, Magic Joe's mouth-watering gooey fruit cake and a pot of elderflower tea and walnut shell cups. Everybody settled down to have a feast. Saley and Galey joined them after taking some water and carrots down to the two deer. The goblin was asleep, curled up at the foot of the tree.

Alex had been very quiet for quite a while now. He seemed to be sitting apart from the others and was looking distracted. Magic Joe noticed this and gently took him to one side.

'What's the matter Alex?'

'I'm not sure really,' he replied. 'I feel so confused. The thing is, that goblin was simply so evil, so cruel and so disgusting. Of course, he does needs punishing. But somehow, I feel vaguely sorry for him now. He must be thirsty and hungry too. But of course, we daren't let him go, but I wonder what will happen to him now... are you going to... are you going to execute him? I'm not sure I could bear that... Or will you lock him up like a real prisoner for the rest of his life. What will happen to him now?'

'These are very intelligent questions Alex,' replied Magic Joe. 'The thing is, my boy, Merry and I have come across some very evil creatures in our time. Don't forget, we have been alive much longer than you. Many, many years in fact. Over the course of our lives we have rubbed up against plenty of bad creatures, most of whom we have managed to vanquish. Some of whom got away. But we do have a rule. We never want to hurt any creature, not even those that want to hurt us. We say to ourselves: *Do to others as you would wish them to do to you*, or as is said in a motto: *Do as you would be done by.*'

'That goblin, for whatever reason, has somehow come to this wood and it is exactly what, in the end, he needs,' continued Magic Joe. 'It was never intended for any creature on this earth to be simply evil. No creature is born truly bad. But somewhere along the way, this goblin has turned really wicked. Yes, goblins as a rule, are cruel, but we don't know why. Perhaps there is a bad streak in them, perpetuated by the parent goblins. Perhaps the little goblins simply learn wicked ways as they grow up. This goblin might have been bullied by his parents or brothers and learnt the bullying way. Or else something else bad happened to this goblin to turn him to cruelty.'

'Merry and I will treat him with the utmost respect. He will be taken care of, fed on nourishing fruits of the forest. He will never again kill living creatures for food. His internal body system will be calmed by what he eats. That alone will help.'

'There will be a good deal of talking, healing, sleep and magic. We will never treat him cruelly, but we will be very firm and not let him try and trick us or fool us. He will have to help us with simple practical tasks so that he feels he has a purpose and is kept feeling healthy. Hopefully, in time, he will find a way back to a different kind of life, learn to be more thoughtful and return to being better-natured,' he continued.

'He might leave here one day or perhaps he might even stay, and become a helpful part of this woodland – eventually. It will be difficult, as he has a long way to go and we will need to keep him under close watch. He will not easily see the errors of his ways. I will stay here with Merry until I am sure the goblin is safe to have around. No doubt it will take some time and effort,' added Magic Joe with a heavy heart. He felt tired. Tired deep down.

'But what about that cutlass?' said Alex. 'Surely that's going to be a big temptation for him, if you give him that back?'

'Yes Alex,' replied Magic Joe, 'that cutlass has magical energies that none of us want around here. That cutlass attracts the darker powers. I personally will do what I can to neutralise them. But it will be a task. Soon, when Ray is quite better again, he and I will fly away with that cutlass and bury it deep into the earth in a remote place, where it will stay until time out of mind. The earth and elements will rust and decay it. Meanwhile, I promise I will personally keep it hidden, out of sight.'

Alex looked relieved. He knew it was the right thing to do for the goblin. Secretly he had felt really uneasy, really uncomfortable, even just pointing his Swiss army knife at the goblin. '*I could never have used it,*' he admitted to himself, and shuddered at the thought of plunging that small knife into anything alive, even a wicked goblin.

Chapter 30

The children gathered around in a group, eating the food, and began to realise that they had come to the end of their quest. They looked at Magic Joe expectantly.

'Well, what happens now?' asked Harry.

Magic Joe looked at the children fondly. 'Well, children, firstly I have to say a huge thank you for your amazing efforts. You were as wonderful as I have come to expect, and did so very well and so bravely. It was a really challenging thing to do, and you acted as an excellent team and with great determination. I can't thank you enough.'

With that, Merry, green woven blanket wrapped around her shoulders, stepped out onto the little deck. Exactly the same size as her brother, she was a pixie-like girl with a mop of golden curls, and pointy ears. She had put on some fresh clothes – a little skirt of tawny flowers, a green mossy cap on her head – and she carried a small basket. Wearing a shoulder bag made of green leaves, she was bare-footed and moved very slowly.

Ray waddled unsteadily after her. He was wagging his tail. He jumped up onto Harry's knee and sat there weakly, allowing his pure white feathers to be stroked. Bella had the rabbit on her lap again and Ellie, sitting cross legged, picked up the squirrel and put it on her lap, stroking it gently.

Merry sat on a little tree stump surrounded

Merry stepped out onto the little deck.

by the family. Hedgy and Nibbler lay curled up at her feet. She looked weak, thinner and paler than the children remembered her from last year. She regarded the assembled group with a grateful smile.

'I need to thank you dear children, you Ray, you beautiful selkies and the kind deer, not to mention you two, Ogo Pogo and Ege Pege.' She coughed and then gathering herself, glanced over to where Aribus and Cornibus, who were nibbling at the grass around the tree.

Merry said quietly. 'I really thought I was done for. You see, I tried very hard to help all the other animals in the woodland here, but I became weaker and weaker as more and more animals fell sick. The enchantment dragged me down. I couldn't look after them all, and I couldn't look after myself. Eventually I was kidnapped here from my own dear little tree house. It got wrecked and very nearly destroyed by the goblin.' Merry paused while she coughed again, shuddering, and then with great effort said, 'I thought I could manage alone. But I was wrong. Very wrong. I increasingly became fearful and full of sadness. Something so precious was violated. My whole way of life. And by the time I realised I did need your help, my dearest brother Magic Joe, it was too late.'

Bea moved over nearer to Merry and put her arm round her to comfort her.

Merry continued weakly, 'Bella and Ellie, you have nursed so many poorly creatures today. You have been magnificent, so kind, generous and loving. You have worked unstintingly to take care of dear little creatures. You took my place and you have inspired me to try again. For this I will give you some of my precious life-giving ointment to take home. Ellie, I give you this little shell of Oak for strength. Bella, the Sweet Chestnut for pain and fear. Remember to use it sparingly and only to help others and yourselves in times of doubt, injury or danger.'

Merry stopped talking and took some deep breaths; she was so tired, it was a struggle to talk. Then she continued, 'Saley and Galey, come here my dears.' Saley and Galey stood up and then kneeled down closer to Merry.

'You, my sweet selkies, have been beautiful

and brave this midsummer's day. You have made a great sacrifice, emerging from your beloved waters to run in this alien, dry, dark and gloomy wood. You have faced danger and dreadful fears with such grace and kindness. I will never forget you or your deeds of such unselfishness. As the day is drawing on, you must want to return to the waters. You must need to find your skins and wrap yourselves once more into them and sink into the gentle world of mermaids, sea songs, and exotic fishes.'

Galey stood up, and in her melodious low voice, said, 'It has been an honour to be with you all this day, and we have had much pleasure in helping the creatures of this forest. But it is true, Merry, we long for our waters now. The day is closing and we will run out of time if we do not make haste and go back into to our seal skins. We must return to them soon or forever be land-locked.'

Turning to the children, Saley added, 'We wish you children all well and will look for you when you are out sailing on the river at Little Japan, or picnicking on the beach at Shingle Street.'

Merry put a small dab of Oak ointment on the two sisters' foreheads and laid her hands on their heads for a moment. They could feel the warmth of Merry's hand spread through them.

Ellie could feel tears pricking at her eyes. She got up and held Galey round the waist in a hug. Saley stood up too and then Bella. The four of them held hands and hugged for some moments.

'I'm going to miss you!' whispered Ellie.

'Go now,' said Magic Joe. 'May all the blessings of the streams, rivers, seas and air be with you. Thank you for your sweet kindness and grace. Now is the time, renewed by sun, to count our blessings one by one. Go safely. We love you so much.'

'Yes, we do!' said all the children in unison, and they too rose and hugged the beautiful selkies.

The selkie girls climbed down the tree, and darting away surefooted, in their light flowing tunics, disappeared into the golden and green woods. The last thing the children saw was a wave of a hand, and a flash of long auburn hair.

Bea and Sophia gently helped Merry back indoors to her bed. They tenderly washed her face and gave her some more drink and soothed her brow with some more oak ointment. Tucking her soft mossy blanket around her, they sat quietly either side of the bed, holding her cold little hands, not speaking but letting her rest peacefully.

Everyone listened and watched as Merry talked outside her little tree house.

Chapter 31

'Well, that's blown it!' remarked Bella, wide-eyed, smiling. 'How on earth are Ellie and I supposed to get back to the beach, your magic tree cave, and the tunnel to get back into my garden. Our seals have just run away!'

'Yes, Bella, that is the next problem to solve,' replied Magic Joe. 'How to get everyone home safely and into the right gardens.'

'Magic Joe, do we actually HAVE to go back to the place we started at?' asked Ellie. 'I really want to go and see my mummy and daddy and tell them all about our adventure. I won't see them for ages, till it's the birthday lunch party and... Oh, I feel a little bit homesick now.'

'Well, Ellie, that makes it all a bit tricky,' replied Harry to his little sister. 'You're supposed to be at Bella's till lunchtime, when Mummy and Daddy drive over to Kettleburgh with some of the party food for the birthday lunch. Do you remember? It was your treat to sleep over at Bella's house last night. Mummy and Daddy would be rather shocked if you suddenly turned up at their house before they've even got up!'

'Oh dear...' said Ellie. 'But I do want to see them, and it IS our birthday weekend. Please Magic Joe... can't I?

'I'll go with her!' said Bella. 'Perhaps Cornibus or Aribus would take us?'

Magic Joe with his head on one side considered little Ellie. She had done so well today, been so brave, kind and good. Nacton village, Ellie and Harry's home, was too far even for a magic deer to run. He thought about the buggy, he thought about the other children. After a long silence, he decided to give Ellie a helping hand. In addition, he formulated a plan that would end up with all the children in the right places at the end.

He pulled out his magic wand from his shoulder bag and uttered a few words quietly. The children looked on wide eyed, holding their breaths. What now?

Soon, at the far end of Merry's tree house deck, there was a great rustling of leaves. And there, swooping elegantly down and landing with a flurry, were the very creatures that Bella and Ellie had dreamed about seeing again. Alberta and Nova, the two Canadian geese. With their vast wing spans and webbed feet splayed out in front of them, their arrival was thrilling. Each goose had glossy brown plumage, with a black head and neck, a white splodge under its chin, black beak, white cheeks, and bright intelligent eyes. The geese greeted Magic Joe, enthusiastically. They loved him for all the kind things he had done for them over the years. They circled around him wagging their tail feathers as he greeted them warmly. Bella and Ellie rushed over and hugged and patted them as well. It was a great reunion.

In a little while, after a good deal of discussion and conferring with the others, the two cousins, their ointment shells carefully placed in their pockets, mounted on the back of the two geese. They tucked their feet in comfortably under the soft wings, Bella on Alberta, Ellie on Nova. The geese took off from the platform and glided away over the tree tops in a southerly direction.

Alex and Harry waved them off from the edge of the platform. 'Bye Ellie!' called out Harry. 'See you later for your birthday lunch – don't be late!'

The Geese glided away over the tree tops.

Riding on the top of the geese again was such a joy for the two little cousins Bella and Ellie. They adored the steady, slow, rhythmic beating of the geese's wings and the gentle warmth of their soft feathers. Everything was so restful; the birds' flying was so level and steady.

As they flew through the blue sky, they looked

around them at the wispy white clouds that floated past. Far below them they could see everything in miniature. Patchwork green fields covered with groups of tiny grazing cows, chimney stacks on the tops of little houses, villages with church spires and little roads with small moving cars on them. It was such a beautiful midsummer's day.

The geese flew smoothly and swiftly. It wasn't long before Ellie could see the top of her house opposite the little green at Nacton village.

'There it is!' she cried excitedly.

Chapter 32

As previously instructed by Magic Joe, the two geese landed smoothly at the bottom of the garden behind the large pine tree where the girls had first met Magic Joe last year. Bella stayed with the geese, patting and petting them, kissing their long smooth necks. Ellie ran like the wind up the garden, as fast as her legs could carry her. With only a tiny click of the latch, she let herself through the French windows and into the kitchen. Kicking off her trainers on the door mat, she glanced at the big kitchen clock and saw that it said 7.00 a.m. She silently ran through the kitchen door and lightly sprang up the stairs to her mummy and daddy's bedroom.

She crawled up the bed, from the bottom end. She wriggled under the duvet, between Joe and Clare, and snuggled up. They were sound asleep. She felt safe and warm. She nudged them both and they moved slightly and drowsily, pulling her to them and cuddling her.

'Mummy, Daddy!' Ellie whispered. 'I've had such an adventure! I helped save Magic Merry. I've been nursing poorly creatures in Merry's tree house which we turned into a hospital. The woods were enchanted by a wicked goblin -' and on she went, quietly telling them the whole story. It took quite a long time.

Joe murmured in his sleep, 'That's spectacular!' He was dreaming that his little daughter was a world-famous surgeon, doing a heart transplant on a frog.

Clare, fast asleep, dreamed that her daughter had turned into a young grey squirrel. She had a bandage taken from a T shirt on her tiny back leg. From the depths of sleep Clare murmured, 'Good little squirrel.'

But neither of Ellie's parents woke up.

Ellie, satisfied with her cuddle, suddenly remembered Bella. She wriggled out of the bed at the bottom again and tiptoed quietly out of the room, glancing back one more time to her sleeping parents.

She ran down the stairs and soon found Bella and the two geese patiently sitting at the back of the pine tree with their tails wagging. Bella had found some chicken pellets by the hen house and was feeding the geese a few at a time.

Bella climbed back onto Alberta, and Ellie onto Nova.

'Thank you, Nova,' she whispered.

'Home to my house at Kettleburgh now please, dear Alberta and Nova. Thank you SO, SO much!' exclaimed Bella excitedly. She too was looking forward to seeing her mummy and daddy.

Once more the geese set off at a run then into flight, across the garden and up over the roof top of Ellie's house in a north easterly direction.

Chapter 33

Back in Merry's treehouse, after the two youngest girls had left, Alex and Harry crept to Merry's bedside, and joining Sophia and Bea, said their goodbyes to her. Merry, slowly rousing herself, sat up, and gave each of them one of the shells of ointment to keep. She told them how marvellous they were, how grateful she was to them, thanking them profusely.

Reaching into her little basket, she revealed the other silvery shells of ointment. She gave Sophia the Chamomile for calming and disinfecting. To Bea, she gave the Lavender ointment for sleep making and relaxing. Harry was given the Arnica to rub on his bruises after football matches. To Alex she gave the Calendula for cuts and grazes. The children treasured the little silvery shells and were thrilled by the gifts. 'Remember to use it sparingly and only to help others and yourselves in times of doubt, injury or danger,' Merry reminded them.

Sophia thoughtfully asked, 'Merry have you got some more for yourselves?' She nodded her head, smiling, and sank back into her little mossy pillow, exhausted. With Hedgy and Nibbler curled up next to her, she stayed safely in her bed, warmed up in her moss blanket. She fell deeply into a dreamless sleep and every breath was healing to her.

After casting a spell to keep the goblin asleep under the tree, Magic Joe walked quietly with the four cousins Alex and Harry and Sophia and Bea.

'..Nature so full of life around them..'

They headed back to the river. Aribus and Cornibus clip-clopped elegantly next to them. Ogo Pogo and Ege Pege were riding on the deer, their matchbox tucked safely inside Harry's pocket. Now, with the forest transformed, the walk was pleasant and peaceful, nature so full of life and beauty all around them.

'Magic Joe,' observed Sophia. 'You seem sad, somehow. Is there something we can do to help you?'

'Yes,' added Bea, 'Is there something wrong, Magic Joe?'

Magic Joe sighed. 'Oh, that's kind of you girls. No, I'm OK really. It's just that I'm rather worried about Merry. You see neither of us are getting any younger and I fear for her living here alone in the woods.'

'Yes, but you'll be here now, won't you, Magic Joe?' asked Alex.

'Yes, I'll be staying here in these woods with Merry for a while now, certainly while we've got that goblin to deal with,' observed Magic Joe. 'But my adventurous nature means that I love to travel about and see new things, experience new places. And of course, I've got my own home next to the river in my little warm sunny tree root cave. All my own possessions are there, and all my own friends around me. My concern is that Merry seems to have lost her delight in these woods, in her own little tree house. I think that what happened with the goblin has really shaken her up, more than we know. I think it's made her feel uncomfortable in her own home.'

'Could Merry go and live in your river side tree root cave, when she's better?' suggested Harry. 'Could you and she live together there? That way you could keep an eye on her and still have your own adventures.'

'Yes, that's a possibility,' replied Magic Joe. 'If I could persuade her to come to the river. You see she loves woods and trees; she makes all kinds of friends with the tree animals, birds and loves the woodland flowers too. She likes to make all those herbal ointment remedies and teas. Did you know she uses beeswax to mix with the essential oils from the flowers to make the remedies – along with a dash of magic! She might not find the plants she needs by the river. And then, it would be rather a squash with the two of us!'

Alex and Sophia were thinking hard.

'Alex, are you thinking what I'm thinking?'

'Maybe,' replied Alex with a smile.

'Magic Joe,' said Alex seriously. 'I know we asked you this a year ago and you said 'No'. But would you consider letting us build a tree house at the bottom of our meadow? Build a tree house for Merry to come and live in, for you to visit whenever you like, where she will be safe and we could keep an eye on her. Where she will be near to Ogo and Ege who live with us?'

Sophia added, 'Bea and I were talking about the tree – oh! – only this morning! You know, that lovely oak tree that needs some work doing on it. The one tucked away secretly at the bottom of the woods where we ended up last year with you?'

'Oh yes, I know it well,' replied Magic Joe. 'It is a very ancient and wise old Oak that has been rather battered and ignored of late.'

'Yes,' said Alex with mounting excitement. 'We cousins could build it with my tools and make it really safe and special for Merry! We could build it exactly how she would like it. It would be so much fun to do that for her. Mummy and Daddy would help.'

'I'll help too!' said Harry.

'Yes! And there are plenty of flowers in the meadow and lots of herbs about in their garden that Merry could use to make her healing remedies,' added Bea.

'Well,' replied Magic Joe smiling. 'That is a wonderful idea. But I would have to talk it over with Merry and see how she feels about leaving Blaxhall woods.'

The little group fell silent again, lost in their own thoughts, and shortly afterwards they reached the river.

There were the stepping stones across it and they could see the old golf buggy sitting there on the other side.

'There it is!' cried Harry. 'Are we going back the same way, Magic Joe?' he asked, while privately slightly dreading the bumpy ride ahead.

Chapter 34

Alberta and Nova gracefully landed behind the oak tree in Bella's garden. The girls patting the geese, dismounted and looked about. There was the hole down at the back of the tree, near the ground, that had sucked them down. It looked much smaller now, just an ordinary rabbit hole with a few raisins scattered around it. Insignificant. The girls eyed it up curiously. Did they really get 'hoovered' down it? Does Magic Joe really live in a beautiful little tree root cave, on the edge of the river Alde, at the bottom of it?

The two cousins, checked their hoody pockets for the beautiful sea shells containing the precious ointment that Merry had given them. Yes, they were still there, and yes! It was true!

They kissed the cheeks and stroked the soft necks of the two smooth feathered geese enthusiastically, thanking them profusely and saying a reluctant farewell.

It was rather sad. The geese waddled away, began to run. Taking off, they extended their beating wings, and smoothly glided up and over the roof top of Bella's house. Ellie and Bella, waving and blowing kisses, watched them go.

The two girls, noticing the glory of the beauty of the morning, walked slowly across the dewy grass. They listened to the birdsong and absorbed the warmth of the early morning slanting rays of sunshine. They were suddenly, more than ever, acutely aware of the joy and delight of this midsummer morning.

They made their way to the back door of the house and entered. Bella glanced at the kitchen clock. It was just after 7.00 a.m. They wearily climbed the stairs. The little cousins were tired!

There was no sign of life from Tom and Dee Dee's bedroom, but they crept in. They had SO much to tell them. Crawling into the warmth of the bed, either side, they snuggled up under the duvet. They felt safe and cosy.

'Happy Birthday, Bella,' murmured Tom, half asleep, as he cuddled his daughter to him.

'Happy Birthday, Ellie!' sighed Dee Dee sleepily, as Ellie curled up next to her.

But before the two little cousins could even begin to tell their story, they had both fallen into a deep dreamless sleep. And Tom and Dee Dee dozed on.

Taking off, Alberta and Nova extended their beating wings

'The glory of the beauty of the morning,'

Chapter 35

Cornibus and Aribus, ridden by Sophia and Bea made their way, trit trot, through the woods back towards Parham. They were followed by the old golf buggy driven by Alex with Harry in the passenger seat. Ogo Pogo and Ege Pege were safely back in their matchbox in Harry's football hoody pocket. The secateurs were in the back. No one was in a rush.

It was a much more comfortable affair for Sophia, who by now was pretty used to the rhythm of movement, and shape of the deer's back. She was pretty confident riding now, and didn't feel she had to hang on for dear life. She patted Cornibus' neck frequently, in her sweetest voice saying, 'Thank you! Cornibus, this is a much smoother ride! I love riding you SO much.'

Bea was sitting nicely poised on Aribus, back straight – a perfect riding position. She was enjoying the journey home as they meandered along the pathways through the dappled trees. It was a truly lovely morning, birds chattering and singing in the branches, wild flowers and bees buzzing around them. She patted Aribus' flank. '*Gosh we are lucky to live in such a place*,' she thought. *'It's been such an adventure! I wonder I'll ever get a chance to ride on a deer again?!'*

The boys were riding along in much more relative comfort than the journey out. Alex had time to avoid roots and stones and they chatted together amicably as they went along.

'Holy horses! That was some monster, that goblin, wasn't he Alex!' exclaimed Harry.

'Not half!' said Alex. 'Did you see the state of his teeth? He could do with a trip to the dentist!' he giggled.

'We did do well, didn't we!' said Harry.

'Blinking heck, yes!' replied Alex. 'But I wouldn't want to go through anything like that again in a hurry!'

And on the boys went, chattering away happily, giving a post mortem on the day together.

Soon they arrived at the perimeter to the grounds round Alex and Sophia's house.

The two deer found a way through the hedge near the pond. They trotted away down through the lovely meadow towards the oak tree at the bottom.

They trotted down through the lovely meadow.

Alex steered the buggy round the ditch and up a small path through into the garden. Cutting the engine, He and Harry quietly pushed the buggy the last bit towards the shed where it was kept. Alex looked at the state of the buggy.

'Golly, I'll have to try and give that a clean before Dad sees it!' he thought.

They took the tools, back into the potting shed, sliding the lock shut. They took the backpack and scarpered down through the meadow towards the oak tree. Harry glanced at his watch. It was just after 7 a.m.

The two girls had dismounted and, saying fond farewells, were patting and hugging the two deer, kissing their noses and stroking their ears.

'Please come and see us again,' Sophia whispered.

Cornibus and Aribus lowered their antlers and bowed to the four children.

'It's been a pleasure to be with you today, children. You have done well. Now we must be off, but we will see you again – one day.'

And with that they bounded lightly across the bushes, dodged the nearby trees and galloped gracefully away across the meadow.

Ogo Pogo and Ege Pege were beginning to make some high-pitched squawking sounds from inside Harry's hoody pocket.

'Oi, let us out!' they squeaked.

'Oops!' replied Harry. 'We nearly forgot about you two.' Harry put the matchbox down on a nearby tree stump and the two miniature pixies jumped out.

'Well, really!' squawked Ogo Pogo.

After a pause, Ege Pege added, 'It's time for us to go now. Next time you need saving, just let us know and we'll be there!'

The children crowded around the tiny pixies, thanking them. The boys stroked their minute wizened hands while Sophia and Bea tried to plant a kiss on their little wrinkled cheeks, (which was difficult as they were only the size of raisins).

'Hey! Get off!' squeaked Ogo Pogo. 'That's quite enough of that!'

And with that, they jumped back in the matchbox, slid the lid shut and took off in the direction of the house through the trees.

The children slumped down with their backs to the old oak. They were exhausted! They pulled out their beautiful little silver ointment shells full of the beeswax ointment, examining them carefully. *'They are amazing,'* thought Sophia.

The children sat quietly with their own private thoughts, listening to the sounds of the beautiful morning.

They were just ruminating and thinking about their day when they heard a familiar shout, 'Ho there! children!'

Rose and Jon, Alex and Sophia's mother and father, were sauntering down the meadow path in their pyjamas. Rose was holding a tray of steaming mugs and called to them.

'Is everyone okay down here?' she asked. Have you all had a super midnight feast? Did you see the sun come up? Hope it was spectacular! I've brought you some hot chocolate.'

'Ooh, yummy!' said Harry with feeling.

'Well Mummy, it's quite a long story,' began Sophia...

...'Not really much to talk about,' interrupted Alex, giving his sister a nudge. 'But yes! It was great fun, wasn't it everyone?' The children all nodded obediently.

Rose looked at them all suspiciously. There was something they weren't telling her! Never mind. She shrugged her shoulders.

Jon surveyed the four children sitting against the oak tree.

'By the way, children, Mummy and I have been talking,' Jon said. 'We think it's high time we did something about this dear old oak tree. It needs some renovation work. You know, cutting out the dead branches and dead wood etc., cutting down the weeds and the undergrowth. Clearing some more space around it. Then when that's all done, over the next few weeks, we wondered if you would like to help us make a tree house in it, for you all to play in?'

The four children all looked at each other nodding vigorously, with sparkling eyes.

'Yes please, Dad! That's a brilliant idea! Can we help design it? When can we start?' asked Alex eagerly.

'Well what about we make a start this morning, before the big birthday lunch party?' replied Rose. 'No time like the present!'

THE END